El Coro

El Coro

A CHORUS OF LATINO AND LATINA POETRY

EDITED BY

Martín Espada

University of Massachusetts Press ▪ *Amherst*

Copyright © 1997 by
Martín Espada
All rights reserved
Printed in the United States of America
LC 97-22019
ISBN 1-55849-110-4(cloth); 111-2(pbk.)
Designed by Jack Harrison
Printed and bound by Thomson-Shore, Inc.

Library of Congress Cataloging-in-Publication Data

El Coro: a chorus of Latino and Latina poetry / edited by Martín Espada.
     p. cm.
ISBN 1-55849-110-4 (cloth: alk. paper). — ISBN 1-55849-111-2 (pbk.: alk. paper)
1. American poetry—Hispanic American authors. 2. Hispanic Americans—Poetry.
    I. Espada, Martín, 1957–   .
PS508.H57C67 1997

811'.5480868073—dc21   97-22019
                                                CIP

British Library Cataloguing in Publication data are available.

Acknowledgments for previously published poetry begin on page 165.

Contents

Introduction

The Latino community in the United States is clearly a community in social and economic crisis. The best metaphor for this crisis is Proposition 187, the most blatantly anti-Latino initiative in memory, fueled by the racial animus which has always defined the true borders of our existence in this country. Poetry flows over those borders, born in crisis yet transcendent. This gathering of poets is proof of that proposition.

The common expectation is that literature born amid social and economic crisis by nature must be didactic and polemical, obsessed with simplistic affirmations of identity and written in a raw idiom unconcerned with nuance. A survey of the poets included here will frustrate that expectation. The work of Latino poets today is more remarkably complex and diverse, beautiful and powerful, than has been previously acknowledged. We can hear echoes of voices from all the Americas: Neruda and Paz and Julia de Burgos, but Whitman and Williams too.

To be sure, here we will find the open expression of anger and grief. There is the music of protest. There is the search for a reflection of one's face after the mirror is broken. But there is also self-mocking humor, the quiet assertion of dignity and the raucous celebration of survival, not only in the individual but also in the collective sense. There are references here to stoop labor and welfare offices and the housing projects of Avenue D, but there are also poems about the Four Horsemen of the Apocalypse and the Minotaur. Among the poets are former farmworkers and gang members, a practicing physician, an ex-tenant lawyer, two professional chefs, various teachers, a mother on welfare, a former professional boxer, and a Vietnam veteran. Several served time in prison; one poet was a political prisoner for six years. Another staged a famous hunger strike; still another was indicted for her work on behalf of Central American refugees. The eldest poet was born in 1904, the youngest in 1977.

El Coro originally appeared as a special section of the *Massachusetts Review* (Vol. 36, no. 4), and thanks are due to the editors and staff of that journal. The issue quickly sold out, giving rise to the idea of reprinting *El Coro* as an anthology, expanding the collection to include many more poets and poems, providing a showcase for new Latino poetry, almost all previously unpublished.

"Latino," for the unfamiliar, refers to people of Latin American origin or descent living in the United States. "Latino" is a term that emerged directly from the community, Spanish in derivation, likely a shorthand form of "Latinoamericano." As with any umbrella term, "Latino" is insufficient; thus, the phrase "Latino and Latina" appears in the subtitle of the anthology to explicitly acknowledge both male and female.

"Latino and Latina," in this volume, includes not only the expected Chicano and Puerto Rican poets, but also Cuban, Dominican, Panamanian, Guatemalan, Nicaraguan, Bolivian, Chilean, and Argentinean poets: forty-three in all. The majority were either born here or arrived in this country at an early age, and thus write in English, with code-switching into Spanish.

Also included in *El Coro* is the poetry of the Latin American exile or expatriate. To exclude such poets, or any poet who came to adulthood in Latin America and may long to return some day, would be to exclude many who live in the United States but write in Spanish, and Spanish-language writers are all too often shunned in this country. Poets such as Marjorie Agosín of Chile and Víctor Montejo of Guatemala make their homes in the United States, write in Spanish but have their work translated into English for U.S. audiences, and even write about events in this America.

Another unusual characteristic of this anthology is its regional emphasis. This is, to my knowledge, the first collection of Latino literature with a special focus on Latino writers living in New England, particularly in Massachusetts and Connecticut.

This focus is a reflection of evolving demographics, a slowly cresting wave of Latino immigration into New England which has gone virtually unacknowledged. Many came, years ago, as migrant farm labor, to work the shade tobacco of the Connecticut River Valley. Others came to serve as industrial labor, working in factory towns such as Willimantic, Connecticut, known as "Thread City" for the thread mills there. Now, there is little opportunity of any kind, with both industry and agriculture severely eroded. The thread mills have shut down in Willimantic; young men now find solace at the local boxing gym. Recent statistics on the Puerto Rican community show that the poorest Puerto Rican barrios in the country are found in central and western Massachusetts. In Holyoke, there is a bright, blinking sign of desperation: the community seeks salvation in the rumored advent of casino gambling. Yet, Latinos keep migrating to New England, often seeking low-cost rental housing or a reunion with family. And there is always that teasing, flitting phantom, the hope for a dramatically improved life, through labor, which is the immigrant's reason for being.

In the Connecticut River Valley, from Hartford to Springfield, that hope manifests itself in the rising number of Latinos attending two-year community colleges, a working-class crowd squeezing through the basement window of higher education. This experience echoes in *El Coro* through the poems of Gary Soto, a Chicano from California writing about his own junior college experience a full generation and thousands of miles away. Asked by a teacher to imagine the lava of Pompeii, the young Soto envisions a tamale in *mole* sauce, "my only reference / to a thing that got smothered."

Now a Latino literary presence has emerged in New England as it once did in California, an indicator of the community's cultural health. Some of these writers are deeply involved in the community: Naomi Ayala of New Haven dedicates herself to working with writing programs for Latino youth; so, too, does Enid Santiago Welch, bringing poetry to the children of a Chicopee, Massachusetts, public housing project. Bessy Reyna is the force behind a Spanish-language community newspaper in Connecticut; Dr. Rafael Campo ministers to Latino patients in Boston.

For many years, there has been a visible, thriving Latino literature in the United States. At this point, contemporary Latino writers face various challenges: they must reject formula, the hollow imitation of a previous generation, the indulgence in their own, distinctly Latino clichés, the temptation to indulge in political rhetoric, the ironic exclusivity of a Latino canon.

Latino poets have always stressed both a cultural identity and a political sensibility in their work, addressing the Latino community as a primary audience. However, today these poets are willing to explore virtually any subject, reaching out to an increasingly wider audience. Of course, Latino poets cannot afford to compromise their work for the sake of having that work reach the larger Anglo audience, demonstrating an eagerness to assimilate—resorting to Horatio Alger tales with a Spanish accent—or, conversely, portraying themselves as authentically primitive, exotic, child-like.

There is indeed a Latino publishing "boom," yet the boom has not benefited most Latino poets, and the publishing industry still refuses to hire Latinos. There is a new openness on the part of literary organizations and private foundations, yet there are also the familiar practices of tokenism and paternalism, along with the occasional expression of overt racial hostility. This is a bewildering moment in history to be Latino and a poet. As one Cuban writer said to me: "If you get it, it's because you're Latino. If you don't get it, it's because you're Latino."

Still, the poetry comes, with an urgency that drives the poem onto the page, at 3 AM if necessary. Not only does the poetry insist, banging on the window at 3 AM, but the poetry insists on being *Latino*. What makes it Latino poetry, beyond the surname of the writer? The work in *El Coro* demonstrates not only the enormous diversity of Latino poetry, but also the common themes and passions of that poetry.

Though Latino identity is no longer the overwhelming preoccupation of the poets, that identity remains a significant theme. Identity is celebrated in poems such as "Psalm for Bacalao" by Jack Agüeros, a homage to Puerto Rican–style codfish: "Lord, thank you especially for bacalao / since it doesn't swim anywhere / near Puerto Rico." Sandra María Esteves recognizes the African and Native American roots of the identity with "In the Beginning," a poem where the gods are musical instruments, from the conga to maracas. Note the signifiers: food and music.

Celebration aside, the poetry confronts painful realities of Latino identity. There is the strong sense of isolation and alienation from mainstream culture. In the words of Julio Marzán, "Next spring I will be / Forty years a foreigner." There is also the battle with the overwhelming pressures of assimilation, the feeling that something is being lost, especially Spanish. Demetria Martínez expresses this feeling in "We Talk about Spanish," where black beans and political activism are not enough to ward off doubt.

When Anglo poets contemplate "language" in their verse, they mean English; Latino poets mean English and Spanish. Julia Alvarez, born in the Dominican Republic, recalls her mother's advice to "write it the way it sounds" for the Spanish "tos" or "vaca," advice that no longer worked for the English "cough" or "heifer": "silence seemed the only way not to be wrong / about the world." Rosario Ferré's offerings in this anthology include two poems written originally in Spanish with her own English translations, plus a poem written originally in English which ponders the differences between Spanish and English; if English is "like a nuclear reactor," then Spanish is like "navigating / the uterus." Then there are poets like Raúl R. Salinas and Víctor Hernández Cruz, who leap gracefully back and forth between English and Spanish within the poem, demonstrating the creative possibilities of bilingualism. Note how Salinas makes the Spanish word "sentado" (sitting) accessible to non-Spanish speakers by shaping the word on the page in the form of a chair.

Still, there is no more important context for the multiracial Latino experience than the borders of racism. The theme recurs in the poetry. Leroy Quintana remembers "What It Was Like" for a truck driver named Antonio, "who could handle a / rig" better than anyone: "Too bad he's a Mexican was / what my tío said the / Anglos had to say / about that. / And thus the moral: / Where do you begin if / you begin with if / you're too good / it's too bad?"

The poets also recognize the dynamic nature of racism, the capacity of racist thinking to adapt, disguise itself, and survive. Patronizing liberalism is sometimes the target of the poet's wrath. In "Imperialism," Demetria Martínez recalls a dubious mentor: "She taught me to say what I mean, / though to this day she refuses / to hear what I mean. . . . Trouble, trouble, educating / coloreds. Those years I picked / your tobacco and you botched / my lungs." Julio Marzán, with angry humor, recalls meeting "The Translator at the Reception for Latin American Writers," who learns that the poet is merely a product of "Puerto Rico and the Bronx": "Understandably he turns, / catches up with the hostess, / praises the uncommon quality / of her offerings of cheese."

But the poets do not spare themselves, their families, or their community in matters of racism. The speaker in Rosario Ferré's poem "The Shadow of Guilt" asks, "Mother, why do blacks / go around the house barefoot?"—because they were born in the jungle, Mother replies—and then contemplates the dark color of her servant, "the perfect way his skin blended in / with the Packard." Elizabeth Pérez recalls, with rueful irony, the discovery of a slave ancestor named Asunción, from Haiti by way of Cuba, though family folklore had transformed her into Congolese royalty.

Indeed, the history of Latin America inspires and haunts Latino poetry.

Frank Lima writes of Cortés, Moctezoma and the conquest of México in "'The Blood of the Chieftains Ran Like Water.'" Rick Kearns, in "Aurelio's Vengeance, Puerto Rico, 1901," evokes the historical struggle between patrón and peasant. Even when distant history is not the focus of the poet, the elegiac voice remains, the poetry singing to, and for, the dead. Both Raúl R. Salinas and Gioconda Belli write of pilgrimage to the cemetery. Marjorie Agosín laments the disappeared.

Another inheritance of Latin America is a streak of surrealism in the poetry. The poems of Clemente Soto Vélez and Juan Felipe Herrera are intensely dreamlike, jarring, dense thickets of images, full of thinking, feeling trees. There are surrealistic moments, too, in poems by Pedro López Adorno, Ana Castillo, Alicia Borinsky, Víctor Hernández Cruz, Dionisio Martínez, and others throughout *El Coro*. There is a strange clarity to this surrealistic voice; the images are indelible, even if in some cases the meaning is not readily apparent. In all cases, the poets challenge conventional notions of language, reality, and the imagination.

The Latina feminist perspective is also in evidence here. The speaker in the Sandra Cisneros poem "It Occurs to Me I Am the Creative/ Destructive Goddess Coatlicue" asserts her independence from the usual expectations: "I am anomaly. Rare she who / can't stand kids and can't stand you." Julia Alvarez recalls the repressive gender roles enforced in a privileged household, "the ringed hand clapped down / on the mouth that might speak / the forbidden thought." Gioconda Belli subverts the standard thinking on menopause, praising the natural transformations of the female body.

Ultimately, this anthology is meant to be *useful*, not comprehensive, exhaustive, all-inclusive. Too many anthologies have the heft of cinderblocks and are as difficult to read as they are to lift. Rather, this is (pardon the pun) a Whitman Sampler of new Latino and Latina poetry. The selections here should, I hope, provoke further reading, study, debate.

El Coro: In many ways this collection of poets is a chorus. Their song humanizes in the face of dehumanization.

Martín Espada
March 1997

El Coro

Pedro López Adorno

LIQUID MATTER

Beer after beer your scholarly ignorance
the Jersey shore
the impeccable beachfront houses at sundown
the flawless dinner jackets
and you an invited dinner guest without a tie
looking for the womb of the matter among the pebbles
since the voices of "global wisdom" at Princeton U couldn't
deliver it

beer after beer flashes of a long-haired paradise
the amazon kisses only dreamed
whispering and swimming towards a face
that launched a thousand words
and one
the very first day the last

beer after beer an intellectual consolation
an international studies' lesson in good behavior
in an underground bar
where the urgency of the moment
chose to ignore you or (at best)
hurled your eyes into the dark beer
as if to quench the monstrosity of the thought.

TALKING TO THE WAVES

I am now talking to the waves. Hissing as in
an endless chant or enchantment. I am now
blowing long-gone kisses to the wind of my
500-year-old journey through the
promised land. Let them come.
I've been patiently gathering my weapons. Rescribbling
the limits of perfection left in the foliage
of the cowcanes; describing without
words the immaculate sunsets west of Ponce. I am
becoming one with the scent of my muse which
(for lack of a better word) is indelibly rumbaesque
or rubenesque in the spumes of this exodus.
I am now talking to the waves. I have
been getting ready with the cunning and compulsion
of a ninety-seven-year practicum behind a veil
of ink that, originally, belonged to Prospero
proper. Now it's mine.

Yet the homeland remains muffled among the mangroves
I longed for as I speak.

VOYAGE

By bus
from Newark to South Orange
a mere thirty minutes of expansionist and competitive
                    behavior
forgotten by the unattended lawns and dogwoods
              the voiceless victims and ransacked booths

in the disorder of interrogations
the streets assume the stench of post-historical consciousness
always blossoming
where many tongues
simply fall off

I self-
    displayed slave of Prospero's grammar
become the lackadaisical performer
              the quarantined consumer of words
while the unknown ones near me
imagined in the comprehensible corrosion
in the tiny church-like structures
whereby the dead bury us with dungs of light
condescendingly   lamentably   or fortunately
(depending on how one looks at it)
philistinize my willing suspensions of disbelief
not wishing to read what I've taken the pain
              to palimpsest

instead one by one they
                    vanish
possibly saving me from hell
or saving themselves from the immurement
of the syllables

the labyrinthine victim and the poem
summoning the end.

Marjorie Agosín

LOS DESAPARECIDOS

Los desaparecidos llegaron a los
muelles, se anclaron
en la redondez del agua,
uno me entregó una mano
otro me encendió el cigarrillo para las futuras travesías
los desaparecidos llegaron al café
de la esquina
donde siempre hablan del amor y la paz
porque eran jóvenes de largos sedosos cabellos
ahora rapados, ahora anclados en la herida nefasta de la ira
pero ahí tienen frío, son fantasmas,
nadie los ve ni los cubre.
tan sólo sus madres que duermen el sueño de los justos
con las fotografías arrinconadas en el oído del sueño
se sientan junto al río, junto al sargazo
¿los puedes ver?
tan sólo hacen unos años que
pedían en voz alta un café con leche
ahora nadie los quiere oír
son tan dulces los gestos de la amnesia
ahí está Fiona Friedmann
con sus ojos de estrella judía
la que la violaron repetidas
veces porque era
judía
sí, judía cobriza,
ahí está con el corazón sajado y cantando
ahí está Raúl
el que hacía música con las
cadenas.
yo los veo

THE DISAPPEARED

The disappeared arrived at the
docks, they weighed anchor
in the fullness of the water,
one gave me a hand
another lit my cigarette for future crossings
the disappeared arrived at the café
on the corner
where they always talked about love and peace
because they were young people with long silky hair
now bald-headed, now anchored in the fateful wound of wrath
but here they are cold, they are phantoms,
no one sees them or covers them.
only their mothers who dream the dreams of the just
with photographs forsaken within sleep's inner wavelength
they sit next to the river, next to the gulfweed,
can you see them?
just a few years ago
they asked loudly for coffee with milk
now no one wants to hear them
gestures of amnesia are so sweet
here is Fiona Friedmann
with her star of David eyes
who was raped repeatedly
because she was
a Jew
yes, a copper-colored Jew,
here she is with her severed heart and singing
here is Raúl
who made music with his
chains.
I see them

vienen al café
a la medianoche como lázaros
rodean la ciudad.
pero nadie los ve.
pero nadie los oye.
qué dulce es la amnesia, qué grato es fingir el olvido
qué complicado es esto de la memoria.
Los desaparecidos
regresan a tu casa
ocupan tu lecho y tu
sueño de espumas y enjambres
aunque como son fantasmas son livianos
y no quieren molestar
tienen ganas de acercarse
a la vida
de besarte
y tocarte los muslos.

Los desaparecidos
llegan al sueño del
torturador
por primera vez lo ven vulnerable en su desnudez
lo miran como si quisieran perdonar
¿pero los muertos a quien perdonan?
es esto asunto de los vivos
los desaparecidos llegan
te piden memoria
café con leche
pan con mantequilla una canción.

they come to the café
at midnight like lazarus figures
they surround the city
but no one sees them.
amnesia is so sweet, how pleasant it is to pretend to forget
matters of memory are so complicated.
The disappeared
return to your house
and occupy your bed and your
dreams
although they are phantoms and weightless
and don't want to disturb
they feel like approaching
life
kissing you
and touching your thighs.

The disappeared
arrive at the dream of the
torturer
and see him vulnerable in his nudity for the first time
they look at him as if wishing to pardon him
but who do the dead pardon?
this is a matter for the living
the disappeared arrive
they ask you for a memory
for coffee with milk
bread with butter and a song.

Translated by Celeste Kostopulos-Cooperman

Jack Agüeros

PSALM FOR BACALAO

Lord,
thank you for bacalao,
thank you for salted bacalao
and thank you for boneless bacalao
and thank you for bacalao
which is so amenable that
it swims in tomato sauce as happily
as it swims in olive oil.

Lord,
thank you especially for bacalao
since it doesn't swim anywhere
near Puerto Rico.
Thank you for making it go good
with green bananas
onion rings and scrambled eggs.

And Lord,
since it's a fish
thank you for letting it fly
to Puerto Rico, thank you
for letting it ride on boats
into our harbors, thank you
for letting it swim in our happy mouths.

SONNETS FOR THE FOUR HORSEMEN
OF THE APOCALYPSE: LONG TIME AMONG US

I. Sonnet For The Elegant Rider

The way I get it is, that when the world is about to end
Four horsemen will come thundering down from somewhere.

One will ride a red horse, and his name will be War.
One will ride a white horse and his name I don't get
since it's Captivity. Does that mean slavery? I don't
want to guess about these things, but translations can
be treacherous. One will ride a black horse and be named
Famine. I get that. Now here's another part that leaves
me scratching my head—one will ride a pale horse, and
since when is pale a color? He is named Death, and I
think this translator has him on the wrong horse. Death,
I know, rides the white horse, which symbolizes his purity.

You see, the future tense is wrong, since nothing is as now, or
as inevitable, or so personally elegant and apocalyptic as Death.

II. Sonnet For You, Familiar Famine

Nobody's waiting for any apocalypse to meet you, Famine!

We know you. There isn't a corner of our round world
where you don't politely accompany someone to bed each
night. In some families, you're the only one sitting
at the table when the dinner bell tolls. "He's not so
bad," say people who have plenty and easily tolerate you.
They argue that small portions are good for us, and
are just what we deserve. There's an activist side to
you, Famine. You've been known to bring down governments,
yet you never get any credit for your political reforms.

Don't make the mistake I used to make of thinking fat
people are immune to Famine. Famine has this other ugly
side. Famine knows that the more you eat the more you
long. That side bears his other frightening name, Emptiness.

III. Sonnet For Red Horsed War

Obvious symbolism; let's call it blood colored; admit
War jumped the gun on the apocalypse a long time ago.

Isn't it shy Peace that deserves free transportation?

What horse would Peace ride? Peace is usually put on a
Dove, but is so rare it ought to ride the extinct Dodo
of lost feathers we infer, and song we also never heard.

War is vulgar, in your face, and favors harsh words,
rides recklessly, and lately has even learned to fly;
drops pink mushrooms, enjoys ugly phrases like body
count and megacorpse. Generals love War, worship it by
sanctifying pentagons. When War shakes your hand, he
rips it from your arm; shoot and burn is his lullaby.

Like Kronos, War dines napkinless on his raw sons or
any burned flesh. Look, War is apocalypse all the time.

IV. Sonnet For Ambiguous Captivity

Captivity, I have taken your white horse. Punctilious
Death rides it better. Dubious, I try to look you in
your eye. Are you something like old time slavery, or
are you like its clever cousin, colonialism? Are you
the same as "occupied," like when a bigger bird takes
over your nest, shits, and you still have to sweep? Or
when you struggle like the bottom fish snouting in the
deep cold water and the suck fish goes by scaled in his
neon colors, living off dividends, thinking banking is
work? Captivity, you look like Ireland and Puerto Rico!

Four horsemen of the apocalypse, why should anyone fear
your arrival, when you have already grown grey among us
too familiar and so contemptible? And you, Captivity, you

remind me of a working man who has to be his own horse.

Miguel Algarín

NUYORICAN ONE WING OLIVE-SKIN ANGEL

He came at Mitch late in his sleep,
there was no stirring of the air,
because, as he said,
one wing does not stir up heavenly air,
thus his movement avoids
whipping up sand storms and wind torrents.
He wears sandals with long leather strips
wrapped around his calves,
he has a tattoo of a Nubian boy
at the top of his right calf, behind the knee,
he said, "the boy's my inspiration and love."
His long black hair covered his olive skin.
He said "I love to visit people because
my one-wing sweep never causes
emotional disturbances or fright."
He began to spin on his right leg
and as he turned, leaves, twigs, herbs
shot out, dropped and grew in his hair.
He said, "harvest these balms from my body,
drink, eat, cure your wounds
and give thanks for what grows on me."
Mitch trembled with desire and need,
yet to touch the olive-skin Angel seemed too selfish.

Julia Alvarez

THE WAY IT SOUNDS

Write it the way it sounds, Mami always said
when I asked how to spell *tos* or *vaca.*
It worked until we came to English
and a cough was not written like it sounded;
a heifer or house or heart, for that matter,
impossible to get right. And so for a while
silence seemed the only way not to be wrong
about the world . . . to hold out
for what was lost: long days filled
with the eternal waving of the palms.

The voice low over the sad parts, breaking
where it cannot pass easily into description,
the voice breathless with the story of its life,
peaking in disbelief. *Ay sí,* I tell you
that it works in English, too, this listening
and then this writing out the human voice
so that it spells its quiet heart on paper.
Now settled in translation I hear her saying,
escríbelo como suena, every time I write it
the way it sounds, word for word, line by line.

THE DASHBOARD VIRGENCITA

In César Chávez country, one of my young, white students wrote an essay in which she criticized how local Mexican people put the Virgin Mary on their dashboard. "It's in poor taste," she argued, "not to mention kind of sacrilegious."

La Virgen on the dashboard is good taste
if you speak Spanish and believe in God.
Never mind the bumper stickers
or the nodding dog that agrees with everyone,
the showy vans on display on the highway
with seventy-miles-an-hour Salvador Dalis.
That's them, the white folks, who grew up in English
and believe driving is a practicing religion.
They've made their cars into false gods
and think the radio's revelation.
We know Who to thank when we get there.
We know just a couple of years ago
we would have required angels to move this fast.
With the help of our dashboard Virgencita
we'll keep up with them, pass them.
Maybe She'll raise one of her hands
and wave, jangle her dangling rosary
at them like a broken chain.
She'll think of something to teach them a lesson.
And we, we'll have good taste once we've eaten
the fruit of our cheap pickings in their Edens.

THE LOST & FOUND SEÑORITAS

Our horrors were hidden,
folded like linens
in a scented closet.
Sweet señoritas,
the family *santas*,
corseted, girdled
in that tropical heat.
Not just the feet bound,
the pale thigh, bosom,
the swell of the buttocks.
The ringed hand clapped down
on the mouth that might speak
the forbidden thought.
¡Dios santo! ¡La Virgen!
Talcumed & taught
to keep quiet in public,
private-schooled, party-schooled,
a smile for El Jefe.
Sweet señoritas,
our little bell voices
thanking, you're welcoming,
pleased to be helping;
trapped in our treasure box,
pink ballerinas
twirling to waltzes
when you open the lid.
No way out of luckiness!
Only by leaving

our paradise island,
exiled to America,
stripped of advantage,
did we find what we knew
we were missing—
though we were told
we were not—
our pale thighs, buttocks,
our mouths freely speaking
these forbidden thoughts.

RECETA DE DIOS #746
Orquídeas amazónicas

Se agarra un pedazo de luz del alba
y se dobla la punta
dándole forma de bastoncito.
Se le agrega goma
para que prenda la bolita de masa
preparada de antemano.
Con ésta se hará el pistilo.

Se agarra un poquito más de masa
y se le pone tinta verde bajita.
De este pedazo se forma el receptáculo
que se coloca en la parte inferior
de la orquídea.

Una vez cortados los pétalos
se adelgazan los extremos de la masa
con los dedos y se pegan alrededor
del pistilo. Se pintan con colores bajitos,
blanco, rosa, celeste, violeta, agregándole
como gracia unos lunarcitos y bordes oscuros.

Las flores y los moradores del río
siempre se ponen a secar parados
ya sea contra un pedazo de cielo o de masa verde.

GOD'S RECIPE #746
Amazonian Orchids

Grab a little piece of dawn light
and turn it at the top end so as to shape it
like a small walking stick.
Add glue to stick on
the little ball of dough
prepared beforehand.
With this the pistil will be shaped.

Grab a little more dough
and touch it up with a light green color.
From this piece the receptacle is shaped
which is placed as the base
of the orchid.

When the petals have been cut out
flatten them out with your fingers
and glue them around the pistil.
Paint them with light colors,
white, rose, sky blue, violet,
decorating them with a few dots and dark edges.

Always place to dry
flowers and the dark dwellers of the river
standing, either against a slice of heaven
or a mass of green dough.

Se pueden hacer del tamaño
que se deseen con sólo
variar el molde cortador de masa.

La forma normal de estas flores
es de tres sépalos y tres pétalos
sin contar el primero
que cayó en 1542
cuando Francisco de Orellana con sus huestes
irrumpió en mi río.

You can make them any size you wish
just by varying the size of the pastry cutter.

The normal shape of these flowers
has three sepals and three petals
not counting the first one
which fell in 1542
when Francisco de Orellana and his army
burst into my river.

Translated by Joseph M. Rodeiro

Naomi Ayala

PAPO, WHO'D WANTED TO BE AN ARTIST

Papo, lying on a bench on Divine
Street, the divinity of neighborhood
angels kissing open his eyes.
Hymns, hymns for the angels
to whose work-beaten faces cling
the fishing nets of insomnia between the broken
bottles of missed hits at the numbers
store and the traffic going by. Papo,
he has small brown hands
that reach out from his eyes.
With them he smears the pollen
of *amapola* memories, dreams up an entire
town of angels, faces the color of the sun.
Amidst this flowering, he calls
for Ochún, her tight embrace, Ochún,
who has been in hiding. Once,
during a great experiment of will,
Papo managed to pull silver
wings from Miguel's *costado*—
just before Miguel died. He had him flying
through smog, concrete, out to the air
bus he was always missing.
But Papo could not come along with him.
How was he to get back afterward?
Angels have such short life spans.
And, how was he to know?
That night, Ochún greeted him
with blood-red roses,
kissed his small weeping hands,
gave him moon
water from her breasts.
He was sure she'd come out this way again.
He had been waiting politely.

THE NIGHT I WALK INTO TOWN

The night I walk into town
to meet my brother
I'm tripped up
by a car whose wheels rip
through a newspaper
along the white line
of the road.
The black bold
type is bleeding.
I scream
but the bleeding doesn't stop.
At the corner a man who hasn't seen
water, food, gloved fingers
this cold, snow-blowing January
asks how many faces do I see
holding his chin up.
Twenty-five, I say
twenty-five thousand.

REFORM

You know we have always been poor,
always been suspect, the ragwater cocktail
of their bad dreams. And, Rebecca, again they say
they want us to be free. Fuck this, fuck that
stuff of salvation by handout assistance.
They want yet for us another freedom of *progress
in self-sufficiency* while they fingerprint
our hands for food. And, nobody's talking up
our case rationally enough, they say.
Yet these are the times of organized lunacy—
though no one fingerprints them for our tears.
No one fingerprints them for our hunger.
José, where could I be now? Ten miles east
of a hot plate of food? Frankie, what more
can they do? Bodyslam us where your body lay
in the street till we bleed again through you?
How to scratch the eyes out
of the face of hunger's monster, María
when you're too weak to be clear, drowning
slow death by drowning in their filth?
Is it like cooking for eight children?
Half yours, half not your own?
Is it easier than not having enough?
Is it harder than the future?
How will we kick back out of this one?
Who will come for us, Miguel
if we are too broken?
The sign of the cross here's
been waking gunshyless & believing
tomorrow might be the same
as we rub the rosary beads of employment

listings so they may yield.
Anything resembling walls will have to
suffice for a house. Even the coffin of our children's
time-bombed lives the moment they leave our wombs.
And praying's done me personally so much
good, now I bask in the luminosity
of neon, in his rainbow-colored song,
believe one day he too might come for me
like the god of employment—off his information
superhighway
shortcut with the sanctity
of city dump angels beating
their aluminum wings.

Gioconda Belli

MENOPAUSE

I'm not acquainted with it, yet.
But, so far,
all over the world,
women have survived it.
Perhaps it was that our grandmothers were stoic
or that, back then, no one entitled them to complain,
still they reached old age
with wilted bodies
but strong souls.
Now, instead,
dissertations are written on the subject.
At age thirty the sorrow begins,
the premonition of catastrophe.

A body is much more than the sum of its hormones.
Menopausal or not
a woman remains a woman,
beyond the production of secretions or eggs.
To miss a period does not imply the loss of syntax
or coherence;
it shouldn't lead to hiding
as a snail in a shell,
nor provoke endless brooding.
If depression sets in
it won't be a new occurrence,
each menstrual cycle has come to us with tears

and its load of irrational anger.
There is no reason, then,
to feel devalued:
Get rid of tampons
and sanitary napkins!
Use them to light a bonfire in your garden!
Be naked
Dance the ritual of aging
And survive it,
as we all shall.

ACONTECIO EN UN VIAJE DE DOMINGO A LA PLAYA

Llovía.
Nosotros pensábamos optimistas:
El camino se aclarará más adelante.
Seguramente en la playa, el sol.

El parabrisas del carro zas zas.
Neblina en las ventanas.
Arboles envueltos en sábanas blancas.
Gente mojada.
Frío en la carretera.

—Mejor estábamos.en la cama.
El horizonte hacia el lado del mar está todo nebuloso.
Devolvámonos a leer y abrazarnos.—

Giramos:
Entramos a Diriamba.
Todo el pueblo encerrado
guardado de la bruma la llovizna.

En el enredo de las esquinas
desembocamos de improviso en una rotonda:
Un monumento nombres de compañeros.
El cementerio al fondo.
Se veía hermoso.
Niebla suavizando la muerte.

—Bajemos. Nunca he estado aquí.
Quisiera ver la tumba de Ricardo Morales.
Dejarle algunas caricias sobre la tierra.
Unas hojitas de limonaria.—

IT HAPPENED ON A SUNDAY TRIP TO THE BEACH

It was raining.
We were optimistic:
it would be clear farther down the road,
sunny, for sure, at the beach.

The swish, swish of the windshield wipers.
Foggy windows.
Trees wrapped in white sheets.
People soaked to the skin.
Cold on the highway.

—We'd be better off in bed.
The horizon over the sea is thick with clouds.
Let's go back and read and embrace each other—

We turned.
Entered Diriamba.
The whole city locked
in mist and light rain.

In a maze of streets
we suddenly found ourselves at a traffic circle:
A monument, names of comrades.
The cemetery in the background.
It looked beautiful.
Fog softening death.

—Let's get out. I've never been here.
I've always wanted to see the grave of Ricardo Morales
and leave him a gentle message:
a few leaves from a lemon tree—

Bajamos.
Las tumbas de los ricos imponentes a la entrada.
Sus ángeles llorando lágrimas de lluvia.
Llovizna y tumbas buscando a Ricardo.
¿Dónde estará Ricardo?
Y encontramos lápidas de otros:
combatientes, padres, hermanos, monjas octogenarias.
Hasta una mezquita oriental con este epitafio:
"Aquí yace Ramón López
que murió joven
disfrazado de anciano."
Pensamos en la muerte.
Yo, Ricardo, buscaba tus ojos.
Aquellos que unas pocas veces vi, inolvidables.
Los ojos de tu hija, Doris María.

No te encontramos.
Regresamos bajo la llovizna pertinaz.
Fue como tocar la puerta de tu casa y no hallarte.
Como que alguien dijera que habías salido,
que andabas en alguna reunión.
Fue como saber que tu tumba no existe,
que andas por allí,
apurado entre las calles mojadas
trabajando sin morirte nunca.

We got out.
The imposing graves of the rich at the entrance.
Their angels crying tears of rain.
Light rain and graves as we searched for Ricardo.
Where could Ricardo be?
And we found the gravestones of others:
combatants, fathers, brothers, nuns, eighty-year-olds.
Even a little mosque from the East that bore this epitaph:
"Here lies Ramón López
who died young
disguised as an old man."
We thought about death.
As for me, Ricardo, I was looking for your eyes.
The unforgettable ones I saw just a few times.
The eyes of your daughter, Doris María.

We didn't find you.
We left under the persistent rain.
It was like knocking on your door and you weren't at home.
Like someone telling us you had gone out,
that you were at some meeting.
It was like knowing your grave doesn't exist,
that you're out there,
walking quickly through the wet streets,
working without ever dying.

Translated by Steven F. White

Alicia Borinsky

TRAICIÓN

El pelo que encontré en tu café
atravesó la ciudad para encontrarse conmigo
vino en un repasador en la manga del mozo
en la caja de azúcar

el pelo casual el que no viste
el lustroso burlón indudablemente sucio pelo
solitario es juez sabe que nada diré

te dejo acercar los labios a la taza
te miro a los ojos
secreteo guiño distraídamente elijo considerar
la lluvia la ventana esta luz aquella pareja.

BETRAYAL

The hair that I found in your coffee
crossed the city to find me
it came on a dishcloth on the waiter's sleeve
in the sugar bowl

The stray hair that you did not see
the lustrous joke undoubtedly dirty hair
alone is judge knows that I will say nothing

I let you put your lips to the cup
look into your eyes
whisper things wink decide to watch
the rain the window this light that couple.

Translated by Cola Franzen

OCUPACIONES DE LA CRÍTICA
a José Emilio Pacheco

el concierto de la gallina
atrae un público de huevos
están contentos de no tener que cantar
aprenderán rápidamente la lección

y un día serán ellos los ridículos
nos entretendrán con su esperanza
desde cerca criticaremos sus esfuerzos
celebraremos su no haber caído aún
compararemos plumas, notas, sangres.

THE CRITICS' TRADE
to José Emilio Pacheco

the hen's concert
attracts an audience of eggs
happy they don't have to sing
they'll learn the lesson in no time

and one day they'll play the fools
entertaining us with their hopes
from close up we'll criticize their efforts
celebrate their not having failed yet
compare feathers, notes, pedigrees.

Translated by Cola Franzen

Rafael Campo

THE LUXURY OF REGRETS

To everyone who died while I was free:
Accept these lines as an apology.

It was unbearable, the joyful feasts,
The robins' eggs in children's tiny fists,

The newspaper rustling on the porch—
While in the photographs, your tongues looked parched,

Your children's bellies hard as ostrich eggs,
Your dead laid out, those spindly arms and legs.

What more was I supposed to do? Give up
My Trivial Pursuit, my chairmanship?

You must believe me now. Damn you, I cared!
I felt your pain as though I'd not been spared

At all, I smelled your stench in alleyways,
I tolerated all the miseries

Of your existence. Sharing what I could
Was not impossible, but plain impractical.

To all who said I never understood:
I led a life not evil, but not good,

Whose purpose may not ever be revealed.
Please, read—pretend with me that we are healed.

THE RETURN

He doesn't know it yet, but when my father
and I return there, it will be forever.
His antihypertensives thrown away,
his briefcase in the attic left to waste,
the football game turned off—he's snoring now,
he doesn't even dream it, but I know
I'll carry him the way he carried me
when I was small: In 2023,
my father's shrunken, eighty-five years old,
weighs ninety pounds, a little dazed but thrilled
that Castro's long been dead, his son impeached!
He doesn't know it, dozing on the couch
across the family room from me, but this
is what I've dreamed of giving him, just this.
And as I carry him upon my shoulders,
triumphant strides across a beach so golden
I want to cry, that's when he sees for sure,
he sees he's needed me for all these years.
He doesn't understand it yet, but when
I give him Cuba, he will love me then.

SONNET IN THE CUBAN WAY

To make you fall in love with me, I'd curse
Before I'd sing to you; implacable
And elegant, I'd force you with my class
Beneath a music kind of tropical
But mine enough you'd never recognize
Its foreign cadences. O island whore,
I'd stare like moonlight in your eyes,
I'd lie that I don't want you anymore
Then fuck you like Americans know how—
To make you fall in love with me, I'd die
Just near enough to you there'd be no doubt
My feelings are eternal. Dressed in dew,
You'd meekly pardon my brutality,
In love at last, so naked you'd seem free.

Ana Castillo

EL CHICLE

Mi'jo and I were laughing
ha, ha, ha—
when the gum he chewed
fell out of his mouth
and into my hair
which, after I clipped it,
flew in the air,
on the back
of a dragonfly
that dipped in the creek
and was snapped
fast by a turtle
that reached high
and swam deep
Mi'jo wondered
what happened to that gum,
worried that it stuck
to the back of my seat
and Mami will be mad
when she can't get it out
Meanwhile, the turtle in the pond
that ate the dragonfly
that carried the hair
with the gum
swam South on Saturday
and hasn't been seen
once since.

Sandra Cisneros

TANGO FOR THE BROOM

I would like to be a poet if
I had my life to do over again.
I would like to dance with the broom,
or sweep the kitchen as I am

sweeping it today and imagine
my broom is a handsome
black-haired tango man whose
black hair scented with Tres Flores
oil is as shiny as his
black patent leather shoes.

Or, I would like to be a poet laundress
washing sheets and towels,
pulling them hot and twisted
from the dryer, wrapping

myself in the warmth of
clean towels, clean sheets,
folding my work into soft towers,
satisfied. So much done in a day!

Or, I would like to be a poet eating soup
today because my throat hurts. Putting
big spoonfuls of hot soup
into my big fat mouth.

IT OCCURS TO ME I AM THE CREATIVE/
DESTRUCTIVE GODDESS COATLICUE

I deserve stones.
Better leave me the hell alone.

I am besieged.
I cannot feed you.
You may not souvenir my bones,
knock on my door, camp, come in,
telephone, take my Polaroid. I'm paranoid,
I tell you. *Lárguense*. Scram.
Go home.

I am anomaly. Rare she who
can't stand kids and can't stand you.
No excellent Cordelia cordiality have I.
No coffee served in tidy cups.
No groceries in the house.

I sleep to excess,
smoke cigars,
drink. Am at my best
wandering undressed,
my fingernails dirty,
my hair a mess.
Terribly

sorry, Madame isn't
feeling well today.
Must

Greta Garbo.
Pull an Emily D.
Roil like Jean Rhys.
Abiquiu myself.
Throw a Maria Callas.
Shut myself like a shoe.

Stand back. Christ
almighty. I'm warning.
Do not. Keep
out. Beware.
Help! Honey,
this means
you.

Judith Ortíz Cofer

THE TIP

Just days before the crash
that killed him, my father
lost the tip of his index finger
while working on the same vehicle
that would take him away.

I recall my mother's scream
that brought me out of Mann's
The Magic Mountain,
and to the concrete drive
now sprinkled in crimson.
His stunned look
is what has stayed with me.
Shock that part of him could take leave
without permission or warning?
He was a man who hated surprises,
who lined his clothes and shoes
like a platoon he inspected daily,
and taught us to suspect the future. His
was the stranger in a strange land's fear
of not knowing, and not having.

After the doctor snipped the ragged end
of joint and skin like a cigar
and stitched it closed, my father
stared transfixed at the decapitated
finger, as if it had a message for him.
As if he suspected this small betrayal
of his body was just the tip
of chaos rising.

BEFORE THE STORM

Hurricane Luis, Puerto Rico, 1995

We are talking in whispers
about what is worth saving. A box of photographs
is pushed under the bed, and the rendering
of Jesus knocking at somebody's door, a hesitant young man,
that arrived with us in each new house, and another
of his dear mother holding his poor broken body
not many years later, are taken down
from their precarious places on the walls.
We surprise each other with our choices.
                                            She fills boxes
while I watch the sky for signs, though I feel,
rather than see, nature is readying
for the scourge. Falling silent, the birds seek safety
in numbers, and the vagabond dogs cease their begging
for scraps. The avocados are dropping
from the laden trees in her backyard
as if by choice. Bad weather always brings in a good crop
of the water-fruit, she tells me; it is the land
offering us a last meal.
        On the outer islands, the fragile homes of the poor
are already in its jaws, the shelters we see on film,
all those bodies huddled in the unnatural dark, the wind howling
like a hungry dog in the background, make us stand solemn.
In the mainland my family and friends will watch
the satellite pictures of this storm with trepidation
as it unravels over the Caribbean. But I am already too close
to see the whole picture. Here, there is
a saturated mantle descending,
a liquid fullness in the air, like a woman feels

before the onset of labor. Finally,
the growing urgency of the sky, and I am strangely excited,
knowing that I am as ready as I will ever be,
should I have another fifty years to go,
to go with my mother
towards higher ground. And when we come home, if
we come home, if there's a home where we believe
we left one,

it will all be different.

Víctor Hernández Cruz

ISLANDIS

This is the taste of the
Guavas of Hesperides
That converted a sabor
Of eyes on loan from the sun.

Was the Carib isles
The ink in the plume
Of Plato—
In the philosopher's mind
A sandy curve of coast
Stretching into red soil
And sky out into the lamps
Of the Gods.

Mayagüez plain Maya
Before the Castillian Quez—
Yabucoa the town's name is
Singing
A stepping stone to Atlantis—

Spectacular ships entered
The domain of Humacao
Guided by red corals
And the incense of gold
Navigational songs of the nymphs
Spiraling out of sea shells.

Were the coquis ten times
Louder in ages remote
Could they have been

The singing notes
That drove Homer's sailors mad.

Did someone speak of Anacaona's
Hairdo of braids weaved
With gardenias
Taínas threaded live cucubanos
Through their tresses
Sparkling lights through
The nights parallel to Hellenic
Theater girls dancing
In some Roman antiquity of
Cordova—

Let us bow our heads
In silence
Pushed back to the twilight
Of ideas
And with the next Venusian
Light to telegram into
Manatí
Declare ourselves
The kings and queens
Of Poseidon
Wearing crowns of
Bird gone feathers.

THE LOWER EAST SIDE OF MANHATTAN

By the East River
Of Manhattan Island
Where once the Iroquois
Canoed in style —
A clear liquid
Caressing another name
For rock,
Now the jumping
Stretch of Avenue D
Housing projects
Where Ricans and Afros
Johnny Pacheco/Wilson Pickett
The portable radio night —
Across the Domino sugar
Neon lights of the Brooklyn shore

Window carnival of
Megalopolis light
From Houston Street
Twenty kids take off
On summer bikes
Across the Williamsburg
Bridge
Their hair flying
With bodega bean protein
Below the working class
Jumping like frogs —
Parrots with new raincoats
Swinging canes of bamboo
Like third legs

Down diddy bop 6th Street
Of the roaring Dragons
Strollers of cool flow
When winter comes they fly
In capes down Delancey
Pass the bites of pastrami
Sandwiches in Katz's
Marching through red bricks
Aglow dragging hind leg
Swinging arms
Defying in simalacras

Hebrew prayers inside
Metallic containers
Rolled into walls
Tenement relic
Roofs of pigeon airports

Horse driven carts
Arrive with the morning
Slicing through Venetian
Blinds
Along with a Polish English
Barking peaches and melons
Later the ice man a-cometh
Selling his hard water
Cut into blocks
The afternoon a metallic
Slide intercourses buildings
Which start to swallow
Coals down their basement
Mouths.

Where did the mountains go
The immigrants ask
The place where houses
And objects went back
Into history which guided
Them into nature
Entering the roots of plants
The molasses of fruit
To become eternal again,
Now the plaster of Paris
Are the ears of the walls
The first utterances in Spanish
Recall what was left behind.

People kept arriving
As the cane fields dried
Flying bushes from another
Planet
Which had a pineapple for
A moon
Vegetables and tree bark
Popping out of luggage
The singers of lament
Into the soul of Jacob Riis
Where the prayers Santa María
Through remaining fibers
Of the Torah
Eldridge St. lelolai
A Spanish never before seen
Inside gypsies
Once Cordova the Kabala

Haberdasheries of Orchard St.
Hecklers riddling bargains
Like in gone bazaars of
Some Warsaw ghetto.

Upward into the economy
Migration continues—
Out of the workers' quarters
Pieces of accents
On the ascending escalator.

The red Avenue B bus
Disappearing down the
Needles of the garment
Factories—
The drain of a city
The final sewers
Where the waste became antique
The icy winds
Of the river's edge
Stinging lower Broadway
As hot dogs
Sauerkraut and all
Gush down the pipes
Of Canal
After Forsyth Park
Is the beginning of Italy
Florence inside Mott
Street windows—
Palermo eyes of Angie
Flipping the big

Hole of a 45 plastic record
The Duprees dusting
Like white sugar onto
Fluffed dough —
Crisscrossing
The fire escapes
To arrive at Lourdes's
Railroad flat
With knishes
She threw next to
Red beans.

Broome Street Hasidics
With Martian fur hats
With those ultimatum brims
Puerto Ricans supporting
Pra-pras
Atop faces with features
Thrown out of some bag
Of universal race stew —
Mississippi rural slang
With Avenue D park view
All in exile from broken
Souths
The horses the cows the
Chickens
The daisies of the rural
Road
All past tense in the urbanity
That remembers
The pace of mountains
The moods of the fields.

From the guayaba bushels
Outside of a town
With an Arawak name
I hear the flute shells
With the I that saw
Andalusian boats
Wash up on the beach
To distribute Moorish
Eyes.

The Lower East Side
Was faster than the speed
Of light
A tornado of bricks
And fire escapes
In which you had to grab
On to something or take
Off with the wayward winds—

The proletariat stoop voices
Took off like Spaulding
Rubber balls
Hit by blue broomsticks
On 12th Street—
Winter time summer time
Seasons of hallways and roofs
Between pachanga and duwap
A generation left
The screaming streets of
Passage
Gone from the temporary
Station of desire and disaster

I knew Anthonys
And Carmens
Butchy
Little Man
Eddie
Andrew
Tiny
Pichon
Vigo
Wandy
Juanitos
Where are they?
The windows sucked them up
The pavement had mouths that
Ate them
Urban vanishment
Illusion
I too
Henry Roth
Call It Sleep.

Carlos Cumpián

WITH ONLY SMOKE TO COVER ME

Tobacco shag clings
onto rough dry lips, that
moisten as I tongue tip
a hand-rolled cigarette.

Resting half-naked
on the county's
basement floor,
save for a few
white sheets
of rolling paper
to cover me.

I realize from
ankles to knees,
I'm turning sandy
across bound shank
muscles that have carried
me to this bony cell,
where there's nothing to do
—except smoke.

So I wait for my day
before the judge's robe,
and freeze at thirty degrees.

It all started around Christmas,
when guilt flushed through my
fresh-from-the-sweat-lodge mind.

That's why I returned that thick
bright wool Pendleton blanket,
"borrowed" from the fancy gift shop
selling relics of Chief Rolling-
Thunder-in-the-Mountains, from their bogus
nostalgia 19th Century *indio* museum.

Just what was I thinking, *kola*,
that "All my relations, *o' mitakuye oyasin*"
would protect my flat *nalgas*,
until I shambled clear out of town?

kola: Lakota for "friend"
o'mitakuye oyasin: Lakota for "all my relations"

THE CIRCUS

A cougar's howl blasts
out of brass cornets,
matched by blaring bugles,
thunderous trombones,
plus two marching kettledrums
dum dum dumbing us deaf
as six muscle men carry cudgels,
four women wearing less than
what's wrapped in ribbon around
their lances bounce freely alongside
13 elephants that line up, turn, mount
and massage each other,
except grey guys one and thirteen
who represent wrinkled
alpha and omega
cosmic pachyderms
possessing the patois of saints
amid the frantic pulse of these
under-the-big-top idiotics.

Martín Espada

THANKSGIVING

This was the first Thanksgiving with my wife's family,
sitting at the stained pine table in the dining room.
The wood stove coughed during her mother's prayer:
Amen and the gravy boat bobbing over fresh linen.
Her father stared into the mashed potatoes
and saw a white battleship floating in the gravy.
Still staring at the mashed potatoes, he began a soliloquy
about the new Navy missiles fired across miles of ocean,
how they could jump into the smokestack of a battleship.
"Now in Korea," he said, "I was a gunner, and the people there
ate kimch'i, and it really stinks." Mother complained
that no one was eating the creamed onions. *"Eat, Daddy."*
The creamed onions look like eyeballs, I thought,
and then said, "I wish I had missiles like that."
Daddy laughed a 1950s horror movie mad scientist laugh,
then told me he didn't have a missile, but he had his own cannon.
"Daddy, eat the candied yams," Mother hissed, as if
he were a liquored CIA spy telling military secrets
to some Puerto Rican janitor he met in a bar. "I'm a toolmaker.
I made the cannon myself," Daddy said, and left the table.
"Daddy's family has been here in the Connecticut Valley since 1680,"
Mother said. "There were Indians here once, but they left."
When I started dating her daughter, Mother called me a half-black,
but now she spooned candied yams on my plate. I nibbled
at the candied yams. I remembered my own Thanksgivings
in the Bronx, turkey with arroz y habichuelas and plátanos,
and countless cousins swaying to bugalú on the record player
or roaring at my grandmother's Spanish punchlines in the kitchen,
the glowing of her cigarette like a firefly lost in the city. For years
I thought everyone ate rice and beans with turkey at Thanksgiving.
Daddy returned to the table with a cannon, steering the black

iron barrel. "Does that cannon go boom?" I asked. "I fire it
in the backyard at the tombstones," Daddy said. "That cemetery
bought all our land during the Depression. Now we only have
the house." He stared and said nothing, then glanced up suddenly,
like a ghost had tickled his ear. "Want to see me fire it?" he grinned.
"Daddy, fire the cannon after dessert," Mother said. "If I fire
the cannon, I have to take out the cannonballs first," he told me.
He tilted the cannon downward, and cannonballs dropped
from the barrel, thudding on the floor and rolling across
the brown braided rug. Grandmother praised the turkey's thighs,
said she was bringing leftovers home to feed her Congo Gray parrot.
I walked with Daddy to the backyard, past the bullet holes
in the door and the pickup truck with the Confederate license plate.
He swiveled the cannon around to face the tombstones
on the other side of the backyard fence. "This way, if I hit anybody,
they're already dead," he declared. He stuffed half a charge
of gunpowder into the cannon and lit the fuse. From the dining room,
Mother yelled, "*Daddy, no!*" Then the ground rumbled under my feet.
My head thundered. Smoke drifted over the tombstones.
Daddy laughed. And I thought: When the first drunken Pilgrim
dragged out the cannon at the first Thanksgiving—
that's when the Indians left.

Sandra María Esteves

PUERTO RICAN DISCOVERY #12: TOKEN VIEWS
—*for the homeless, Penn Station, December 1990*

We are pictures on a wall
A fine painting of perfect proportions
Appropriately framed
Gilded in silver and gold
Unique expressions pressed firm
Between solid plastic layers
Hanging against a hidden surface
Where we fear to reveal
The secrets of our strokes
The pure color of our screams
Stories captured in our violent eruptions

No, if we're lucky
We hope just to hang
Unnoticed
Out of the way
Quietly safe
Neatly positioned and camouflaged
Amid a finery of French Provincial
Italian Baroque
Gucci and Chippendale

Yes, if we're lucky
No one will notice
The nick in the corner
The tear on the edge
The maligned perspective

Rivers of pain
Streaming from our substance
Causing offense to the properly proud
Who, if they were to suspect
The madness of our common renderings
Would reject us
As easily as a glance
At their voluminous trash.

IN THE BEGINNING

In the beginning was the sound
Like the universe exploding
It came, took form, gave life
And was called Conga

And Conga said:
Let there be night and day
And was born el Quinto y el Bajo

And Quinto said: Give me female
There came Campana
And Bajo said: Give me son
There came Bongoses

They merged produced force
Maracas y Claves
Chequere y Timbales

¡Qué viva la música!
So it was written
On the skin of the drum

¡Qué viva la gente!
So it was written
In the hearts of the people

¡Qué viva Raza!

So it is written.

AMOR NEGRO

In our wagon oysters are treasured
Their hard shells clacking against each other
Words that crash into our ears
We cushion them
Cup them gently in our hands
We kiss and suck the delicate juice
And sculpture flowers from the stone skin
We wash them in the river by moonlight
With offerings of songs
And after the meal we wear them in our hair
And in our eyes.

Rosario Ferré

LA SOMBRA DE LA CULPA

—Madre, porque los negros tienen
la palma de la mano blanca?
—No son como nosotros, hija.
Los trajeron de bárbaros países
y siguen siendo bárbaros.
Eusebia, Brambom y Santiago,
Carmelo, Arsilio y Casilda
andaban en sus ajetreos por la casa.
El silencio de la selva
les acolchaba los pasos,
pero yo pensaba que era
porque no usaban zapatos.
Eusebia, la epiléptica, planchaba
las camisas de mi padre
y dejaba en ellas el sumo
de los pantanos del Africa,
Arsilio regaba las plantas,
Carmelo enceraba las losas,
Casilda brillaba la plata,
y de Brambom recuerdo la manera
en que su piel se confundía con el Packard.
Negros con los pies rosados
llegaban a viejos sin canas,
en las mejillas la noche,
en los dientes la mañana,
y en la mirada la sombra
del tigre que pasa.

THE SHADOW OF GUILT

"Mother, why do blacks
go around the house barefoot?"
"They were born in the jungle, dear,
they don't like to wear shoes."
Eusebia, Brambon, and Santiago
Carmelo, Arsilio and Casilda
were always doing house chores.
Eusebia's skin was a swamp;
her sweat steamed my father's shirts
every time she ironed them;
Arsilio watered the plants;
Carmelo buffed the tiles;
Casilda polished the silver,
and when I think of Brambon, I remember
the perfect way his skin blended in
with the Packard.
Blacks with pink skin on their feet
they grew old without a trace of gray,
wild moss cushioning their soles
dusk falling on their cheeks
dawn breaking in their smiles
and in their eyes the silent shadow
of the tiger lurking by.

Translated by the author

REQUIEM

Teseo se ha convencido al fin:
el Minotauro es su destino.
Se levanta y se ciñe al cuerpo el escudo.
Al calzarse las sandalias, las ajorcas de sus brazos
tañen como relámpagos.
Perniabierto y ciclópeo se cierne sobre Ariadne
y se ajusta al cinto el puñal.
Le susurra al oído que algún día habrá de regresar.
Le ofrecerá entonces una rica cornamente de marfil
transportada sobre cojines de brocado
desde el otro lado del mar.
Teseo la abraza por última vez
y se aleja,
iluminando el laberinto con el brillo de su espada.
Ariadne se apoya contra el muro.
Escruta las galerías con el ojo ahusado,
ahilado en la negrura como un cono de luz.
Una espiga de cartílagos glaciales
se le ha astillado a lo largo de la espalda.
Se desliza hasta encontrar asiento sobre el polvo
apisonado de oscuridad sin fondo.
Un dolor le desgarra súbitamente las entrañas
y siente un vino tibio escurriéndosele por la entrepierna.
Ha comenzado a abortar al Minotauro.

REQUIEM

Theseus is finally convinced:
the Minotaur is his destiny.
He rises and buckles up his shield.
As he straps on his sandals
the bracelets of his arms ring out
like lightning.
Legs apart, Cyclopean, he stands over Ariadne
and resolutely fits the dagger to his waist.
He whispers in her ear one day he'll return
with a rich horn of ivory on a damasked cushion
from across the seas.
Theseus embraces her for the last time
and strides off with a swagger
lighting up the labyrinth with the gleam of his sword.
Ariadne leans against the wall.
A reed of icy bones
has splintered down the length of her back.
She sits
on the stamped-down dust
of nothingness
—no bottom there.
A sudden pain tears at her insides.
She feels the warm wine
as it runs down between her legs.
She's begun to abort the Minotaur.

Translated by the author

LANGUAGE CURRENT

English is like a nuclear reactor.
I'm in it right now.
As I shoot down its fast track
small bits of skin, fragments, cells
stick to my sides.
Once in a while whole sentences gush forth
and slam themselves against the page
condensing their rapid sprays of pellets
into separate words.
Sometimes I travel in it at 186,000 miles an hour,
the speed of light,
when I lie sleepless on the bed at night.
No excess baggage is allowed.
No playful, baroque tendrils
curling this way and that.
No dream time walkabout
all the way down to Australia.
In English you have to know where you're going:
either towards the splitting of the self
or the blasting of the molecules around you.

Spanish is a very different tongue.
It's deeper and darker, with so many twists
and turns it makes me feel like I'm navigating
the uterus. Shards of gleaming stone,
emerald, amethyst, opal
wink at me as I swim down its moist shaft.
It goes deeper than the English Channel,
all the way down to the birth canal and beyond.

Diana García

TÍSICA

Ahwanee Tuberculosis Sanatorium, Yosemite Valley, 1958

What does your dusty shack
in a San Joaquin labor camp
say to this converted cavalry barracks
nestled below Yosemite's Half Dome,

this tuberculosis sanatorium
downwind from Tuolomne Meadows
and the Ahwanee Hotel,
elegant lodge for wealthy tourists.

What you cleaned from the walls
of your shack stayed with you,
the stuff of last summer's tenants,
their dried and caked remains:

uncooked beans, spilled rice,
the shells of roaches plastering
the cracked ceiling and floor.
The browned, yellowed stains

on the mattress troubled you
but sweat and blood betray
a life picking fruit, you thought.
You thought your cough reflected

dank air—mist rising from the creek;
bad air—the outhouse mid-day.
But your skin sallowed, the bags
beneath your eyes deepened.

Consumed by cough and sweat, you wait
as veiled nuns collect your ochered sheets
each daybreak. You approve.
Removed from friends and family

allowed no contact, you bask invisible
in a fine air of pine and wealth,
numbed isolation in a nation's preserve.
You flatten clay, form rows of Half Dome

ash trays, spoon holders, coded messages
urging release. If air alone could rise, sift
dissipate tuberculosis passed
among migrant families, you might have fled

this sanatorium months ago. Instead, you stall
with patients labeled unclean, unclean, sinful.
You hear the whispered tísica, tubercular,
nightmare of the poor, the dread disease.

THE CREEK THAT BEARS THE SALMON

Once upon a time
the creek prowled my town
bearing sleek salmon
headed for the coast.

It tore tomatoes
from Bandini's field,
hung heron feathers
in the tule marsh,
tangled roots of eucalyptus
at its banks.

Its trill threaded trains
along the Santa Fe tracks;
its piping lured bombers
from storms farther north;
its hum hustled rigs
hauling wrist-thick carrots,
tomatoes so ripe
their scent stained
the air.

When the creek sighed
my name below
the G Street bridge,
sang the shape
of my smile
on straw-colored slopes,
I broke for the coast
with the salmon.
When your time comes
to shake loose
from the valley
disregard the creek:
it shifts all the time.

Magdalena Gómez

LA TERRAZA

Puerto Rico came to Manida Street
with the Martínez family
Don Santito saw Aurora for the first time
speckled like a turkey egg
braids touching her thick menstrual waist
as she daydreamed beyond
daddy's finca of cows about how
she would leave her green mother
on the wings of a bird too big to trust
a surprise of tears flooded her blue apron
Don Santito was the man with the handkerchief
trembling with shame of wanting her
who had been born decades after
innocence had left him
she smiled that smile of being seen
amid mountains and meadows
a rooster made himself known
among the hens
Santito eloped with her floating eyes
offering a stick of gum
the cuteness of calves
supplied conversation
as she shifted from foot to foot
scratching one with the other
Santito had nowhere to put himself
asked her name
Aurora.
Aurora?
Aurora.

The farm had been sold to Dole
since Papí's heart had shredded with grief
when Mamí left him for a Monsignor
of the little church made of stones
in honor of Our Lady
it was too much for him
this betrayal by God;
Aurora blew her nose as loud as she could
running her finger back and forth beneath it
to scare Santito away;
he offered her a cherry Lifesaver
and bent to tie his shoe
kissing the length of her feet with his eyes

Papí called to her
for the afternoon milking
of cows swollen with grief
they felt Aurora sink beneath the weight
of a stranger's glance;
they would lose her.

Aurora flew to the promised land
on the wings of a bird
too big to trust;
Papí promised to take care of business
and be ready to give her away.

Santito bought a house
on Manida Street
with used furniture and bodega money,
Aurora had the one room with a view
of wires tangled with trees.

Santito built a terraza
where he hung a hammock
and planted tomatoes and aguacates
in coffee cans,
there was no lack of flowers on the table,
no lack of candles by the bed.

Aurora learned the ways of woman
lost at sea and hungry
the desert ways of woman thirst
the sky ways of the slate colored birds
that cooed but did not sing;
Aurora learned
to cool concrete with memories;
Aurora, swollen with grief
birthed seven more women into the world
teaching them the ways of tasting beans
when there is only rice.

Puerto Rico came to Manida Street
with the Martínez family;
seven women swing from a hammock,
one more awaits her father's return.

Ray González

ÉSE

Ése, I saw you scream
in the brown waters of the barrio,
found you sleeping in the fist
of the polluted moon,
a broken beer bottle
in your heaving chest.
You were my friend
in the story of the tortillas
that fed us, made us fatter
as the border changed course
with the restless river.

I saw you boil the soup
to extract a daze
out of your dagger,
dim fires that masqueraded
as warmth from your cut-off hands,
stumps flying in the blood
of the gang that celebrated you.
You wanted to cross the wire
one more time, mud charted
to flow south toward
your killing dream.

You lifted the mountains
to touch your sweating chest,
carried something in your pockets
of rags and ripped desire.

I last saw you crucified
on the adobe wall as
a brown shadow I surrendered
in a dream long ago.

We were the only ones
who knew about it because
we were in the dirt streets that flooded
when it rained.
We ran ahead of the rising water,
crossed the corners as cars splashed us,
made us dodge the flying mud
as it formed into faces
lying down in the sinking streets.

THE COST OF FAMILY

Everything moves through the corn.
It applies to the wound and the crop of injunctions,
forested backdrops against the tired praise
that will teach me the melody of going up.
Everything grows through the corn.
It means what is not human spoils the power of the sun,
until we can't destroy ourselves without picking
the strongest tortured woman out of the field.
Everything is harvested through the corn.
It means the hard dry husks are nestled in the hair
of the woman who smells like grasshoppers,
the last aunt who guards the sand after
the crop was destroyed by too much hunger.

THESE DAYS

These years the border closes,
mojados sent back to be found as bodies in the river,
or the cut-off head hanging in the tree.
The gang in the barrio where I work sprays
graffiti on my office door, symbols I don't understand.
The English and Spanish don't belong to me.
They vibrate in drive-by shootings,
boys gasping with laughter and the gun,
betting on who will get shot or dance in prison.

Inside a mountain,
a man gets up and wonders what happened to
the *cuento* passed to him about madness
of a family who fled here, building a stone bridge
to hold water that saved them, made their corn grow.
Water seeps into the man's ears when he lies down.
It trickles into the room where he grows old,
water weeping out of the saguaro so he can cup his hands.

The hills contain graves of Mejicanos,
the rumor my father's ancestors were throat-cutting thieves
who died without markers on their graves.
I read about the psychic in the Alamo who encountered
spirits of Mejicanos forced into Santa Ana's army to die.
He contacts Bernardo y Juan Vargas, brothers trapped
156 years as tourists step on them,
soldiers revealing they want to rest in peace.
The psychic asks if the ghost of John Wayne dwells here.
The brothers tell him Wayne wanders among the dead,
never speaks because he can't find
the spirits of the Texas heroes.

I wave to the gang member we hired
to paint a mural on our center wall,
his arms finishing the blue and yellow feathers
on the Aztec face he created,
showing me how the man trapped in the mountain
can find his way out when I enter the old house to find
he is a muralist mixing color from
the burned mirrors under our familiar floors.

Juan Felipe Herrera

APHRODISIACAL DINNER JACKET

In Veracruz, they know how to drink coffee.
Young men roll naked on their backs. On cement.
On the sadism of America.

They pick up their ragged shirts off the ground and receive proper tribute
from the tourists: Palms, guanábana, pámpano fillets in black sauce from
San Andrés where Agustín Lara learned the formula for sadness and
    rhythm.
Where he learned to back up limousines so they could connect all things
in the universe. Here is my cut jaw he said. Here are my tavern strings,
he crooned as María Felix kissed the scars on his neck.

St. Lara.
I keep his candles burning. I keep oil and obsidian
by the wax figure; I tell the story to the lost ones. Follow
the shark tooth of the Malecón where gay Veracruzanos
smoke black Tabasqueños. Whisper into the old men's bar rooms
at the Hotel Ortíz. Sell fat prawn and one hand of rock salt.

I was born there. I was betrayed there twice. Two women.
One from Sinaloa suffering from rape and alcoholism.
The other from Harvard. Caught in a tight habit of perfection
and Marxist Leninism. I was alone there. Full of music

and marimbas, lavish shade, the young hands of dead prisoners
on the Isla de Sacrificios. I stood there. Awakened for the first time.

In the tombs, the cells
and the drip water from the soft arch above me.
I went down into the underground labyrinths, El Infierno, black
Spanish dungeons wet with phlegm and urine. A corner
where I could breathe.

I looked up and saw nothing.
A shaft of light.

A rectangle two hundred meters above me. Every day the sun dripped for
seven seconds. Then I rolled up my arms and punched myself in the testicles,
So l could feel a coolness travel in a star shape through me. So I could kiss
the ground with my entire body, feel the rumble from below. So I could leak
into the gravel and the torn pages and knotted sheets, so I could reach for
the green trousers of Chucho el Roto, so I could escape with him to Orizaba
where we would climb the mountain by Jalapa. Where we would go up in
November, on the day of my mother's birth and seek wisdom from the herb
women. The ones who tossed fire and changed their breasts into pearl,
ascensions and healing stones.

THE ANTHROPOMORPHIC CABINET

They killed the Tlaxcalans. They slaughtered their daughters
and wept only once. When they were satiated with the scent
of Mazapán after their sundry affairs in the harem—
this is when they wept.

Pulled out the robe of their ancestors from Extremadura and wept
aloud, as their banquets resumed in the gardens. I was left behind,
in the palace. In the military dance hall. I called to them once.

I wrote out the name of my gods in cuneiform, in the pink
negative language that I own from my mother, I scratched out
my own contract for transformation.

And yet, they issued the order against me. It was simple and tawdry.
It was as usual. My skin was in their shape now. This was enough.
My skull resembled theirs, except my face was bowed and fell into my chest,
in grayness. My arm resembled a loaf of Spanish bread, my last breast
was held up for exhibition in the Friar's hallway. And my right hip
gashed with a capital letter. My legs folded in an odd fashion.
I could not speak.

Unrecognizable with my hands, with my letters
and the slit below my belly. A rag poured out of my bowels.

How they tried to clean me,
I don't know. A rag spilled out of my back, how they tried to translate
my motion, who can say. The witnesses? The bartenders?

Ask Motolinía, ask Sahagún, ask my masters lurking in these quadrants.
I have their clothes in my box. You can call them and they will ask for
trousers. You can test the case if you wish. Only one arm holds me now.
I can't tell whose it is. It must be mine.

Recognize the strings that shoot from the ulna. I can tell by the tattoo
of a Guacamaya parrot. Sperm and seashells, yellow lines across my cheeks.
These are yours.

FROM *LOVE AFTER THE RIOTS*
3:07 am

Seven black children are being held hostage
by the vested cops. A Korean, an Arab, a Mexican with a broom.
Bicycles and an umbrella with an old woman.
Upside down, she struggles for her face.

No one can go home now. America,
America.

A grandfather man comes out of the building.
That's it, the reporter shouts
and sings Ave Maria.

Norberto James

LAS ESTATUAS
mueren también
si nadie las mira

STATUES
also die
if no one looks at them

Translated by Beth Wellington

ÁRBOL

La caída del árbol le distingue.
—JOSÉ LEZAMA LIMA

Yerta raíz de ausente savia
tu detenido rumbo
y la oscuridad que paces
en precaria verticalidad
se alimentaron antes
del fulgor que ahora de tu piel rebota
Seguirás inadvertido
aunque en la mar del viento giren tus ramas
    tristes aspas desheredadas
aunque en medio del fértil silencio de la noche
resuenen tus sirenas
se enciendan tus faros de luciérnagas y búhos
Cuando muere un árbol
algo de lo mejor de las sombras se nos va

TREE

    Rigid root of absent sap
your halted path
and the darkness you graze upon
in precarious verticality
were once nourished
by the glare that now bounces off your skin
you will continue unnoticed
although in the sea of wind your branches twist and turn
      sad disinherited propellers
although in the middle of the night's fertile silence
your sirens blare
your beacons of fireflies and owls light up
When a tree dies
something of the best of the shadows slips away from us

Translated by Beth Wellington

Rick Kearns

AURELIO'S VENGEANCE, PUERTO RICO, 1901

La luz de la luna,
cuando no mata, inflama.
     —PUERTO RICAN PROVERB

Very early in the
morning in the wet bushes
waiting for the coquí song
to rise crescendo so he
could torch the grand
old
house.
The red mist that
had followed him
through the forest night
had
disappeared.
He was alone. Mind is
drifting
recalling old stories
Rufino the shark killer
defeated sharks in furious
underwater battles with
just a knife and a sacred
totem.

Where is my packet
of yerba buena he
checks his pockets all's well
it's
there he looks to the
river where Hippolito

killed himself as so
many
others so
many faces gone to
the river or hung
themselves from ceibas in the
tiempo
muerto/dead time the
long jobless stretch of
desert after the sugar harvest
zafra/zafra time to
dance and drink and bet
small wages on cock
fights.

The full moon
illuminates the back
of the house he watches
and
thinks I am Rufino I am
the Taínos who discovered
that Spaniards were not
gods
Spaniards could be
drowned and they sat
with the body for 3 days
just
to be absolutely sure.
I am going to burn the
house of this bastard
patrón and the Americans
won't
lift a finger to come

after me they are too busy
too busy some are trying to
help
others are behaving worse
than the Spaniards what
is this word they use,
nigger?

He freezes.
Noise of footsteps across
pebbles it is OK it is
Gabriel stumbling home singing
and farting loud enough to
wake anyone in the house
there is no motion from the house
he
takes the sticks covered
with rags and pitch moves
silently to back of
house
match
torches
poof.

These are
the flames of hell
you bastard you won't
be back to enslave my family any
more nunca
jamás.

JÍBAROS

Jíbaros
in white straw hats
moving through wild
caña that shoots over
the tall grass,

lead spotted horses
past an aluminum
recycling plant

as we pass them
on the road to
million-year-old caves

cut from ancient rivers
in new
old
Puerto Rico.

Frank Lima

"THE BLOOD OF THE CHIEFTAINS RAN LIKE WATER"

Juan de Alvarado's, "Tonatio," "the Sun,"
massacre at the feast of Toxcatl, Tenochtitlan
Florentine Codex, Book xii

July 30, 1995

Moctezoma is drowning
In his own sacred blood
He whispers to Cortés
Who is not there

       where is Hannibal?
       why doesn't Dante speak to me?
       you promised
       for excavating my body

Which no longer exists
Only your allergy to gold

       Cortés Cortés

You leave me
The resonance of steel
From your luminous hand
The short marriage of life
The inescapable kiss of death
Like a pale pink sky
On ornamental corn
Like quiet scallop shells
Folding each other up

Breathing a little smoke
Into the heart
That coughs
Giving life to the sun

Cortés Cortés

Will my avocado trees pledge
Fealty to the king of snow in
Spain?

Will my daughters faint when
They see the naked blood of
Christ?

Why do you want to make our children
Pink rubella
Like the sonic rage in Alvarado's
Eyes?

While their little fists clutch the
Canal in their mother's
Breasts
My bones will turn into the dust of
Flowers
Your bones into the dust of
Fever

Your gold will fly like bees
Across the wet grasses of the sea
With the gliding centuries over our graves

Your god is a giant skewer
Looking for mosquitoes who wait a lifetime
For a pious hand to crush them

        Cortés Cortés

I die alone without you
Without my own sacred blood
With the heart of a dog that
Licks your white hand

        "You have ruined yourselves and me also"

Because studying time and murder
Is the soul of man
The spiteful silence of a dream

        Cortés Cortés

        "as a song
           I was born
              as a flower
              I will
                die . . ."

SCATTERED VIGNETTES (excerpt)

I remember it was a noisy spring in Spanish Harlem when
I came home one evening after running the streets. I found
my mother in the bedroom sitting in front of her Renaissance
Bronx-Italian vanity; her face was glowing with mascara
and rouge. She was wearing large, ornamental, miniature
playground-swing earrings made of gold, and all her
jewelry and her favorite perfume, FALLOW ME: It was a
dark blue bottle with a white decal of a palm tree and
a quarter moon.

Her hair was in what she called her Joan Crawford up sweep,
held in place, in the center, by a large Spanish comb that
was flanked by two long ornate, lethal skewers.

Her eyes were puffy and moist. She looked like a
Chinese emperor with lollipops in her hair. She calmly
faced me and informed me that my father was dead.
Before I uttered a word, she became quite erect and
announced, with an air of glutinous authority,
that the cause of his death was "acute alcoholism."
She almost smiled as if the term would somehow
dignify his condition in Central Park.
As if he were a great casualty of an honorable war.

The fierce caveman in drag was dead.
The warrior who vanquished cirrhotic spirits was dead.

My mother began to drink a lot.
One summer night she was drinking and became ill.
She was glistening with perspiration,
cheap perfume and wrapped in cigarette smoke.
She asked me to help her to bed.

She was wearing a house dress with nothing underneath.
This was shortly after my father's death.
I may have been twelve,
perhaps younger.

She asked me to lie next to her.
I did and fell asleep next to her
with extraordinary anticipation.

When I awoke she was a warm mist hovering,
suspended over me,
naked,
a giant night bird
whose soft long feathers
were sweeping my body away
into the cumulus clouds
of black pubic hair.
My pants were down to my knees.
I looked at her for an instant.
A nanosecond in a boy's erotic time.

She was startled.
I put myself back to sleep.
No, a coma.

    the bells
  in all the children's books
    were broken
  all the shooting stars fell
    out of heaven
  and it was forever darkness
    and sadness
  at night the moon would burn

thereafter
like a rose
that would always belong
to my mother

I had drunk
Medusa's blood,
in the dark,
saw her face,
but,
unlike Perseus,
I became the blind groom
of unfathomable
fascination

After that whenever she began to drink,
I would stay home with her.
She was the moonlight.
She was the darkness.

When my boyhood friends would boast of
seeing so and so's panties,
I would go home to be with my mother.

My first arrest took place in junior high school:
a gun.
My second arrest:
a gun, etc.
I was in a club called
The Young Demons.
We were into guns,
drugs and territory.
My life was rehabs,

Arrests and jails
Crabs
Syphilis
Hepatitis
And finally
The madhouses:
These were the walls of insomnia
Where Dante became incontinent and feeble,
Twirling his eighteen inch Asian penis;
Where God sat in an antique electric chair
Preaching the gospel of a heaven made of iron;
Where doctors and lawyers
Burned their faces with lighted cigarettes;
Where human excrement was soap
And patients removed imaginary wires from their throats;
Where the clouds of heaven could be bought for a blow job.

Demetria Martínez

IMPERIALISM

The lady's British accent
was fake, years later it still
infuriates. Her Cambridge estate
had china, flush toilets, English lessons,
in exchange for chores she taught me to speak
in full sentences, cured me of my accent,
a colored girl's dream, room and board.
She taught me to say what I mean,
though to this day she refuses
to hear what I mean.

Ah, but she'd been round
the world, photographing
revolutions, toasting with Daniel
Ortega, she knew what was best
for a spic like me, nightly I
recited Chaucer by the Greek
column and the peach tree.

Miss, you tap the porcelain teapot,
time for your nicotine fit,
poof smoke away from my
face but we're in the
same windowless room.
All I wanted was the vote,
the right to remain silent,
now you call me ungrateful,
me, writing a new constitution
full of truth and bad grammar.

Trouble, trouble, educating
coloreds. Those years I picked
your tobacco and you botched
my lungs. You taught me to spell
trigger, now I've got your gun.
Run Jane run run run
Lady, dear lady,
the empire
is done.

WE TALK ABOUT SPANISH

Not in Spanish
Dream with dictionaries
Blood-thinners
Marrying out to whites
Damn good black beans
But so what?
Damn good politics
But so what?
Oh there were times
Like in the orange groves
Outside Phoenix
My task was to mark charts
To ask the Guatemaltecas
When was your last period?
And so on as they lined up
To see a doctor in a trailer
And there was that night
in Harvard Yard
When a North Vietnamese
Soldier-poet tested
Spanish he learned in Cuba
It worked
We found a third way
His voice a high-wire
I crossed over to him
Fearless as a spider
If we didn't know a word
We filled in the blank
With a star
It is a light
That years later
I try not to curse

MILAGROS*

after a painting by Francisco LeFebre

When at last you find something worth
longing for

you breed horses again
half Peruvian Paso, half Arabian
dance step and a mane like Rapunzel

you grind hummingbird bones
to a powder, aphrodisiac from before Columbus

your brushes on fire with color

and me? I listen for words that mean *heart*,
collect them like milagros we pin
to the statues of saints
in the church at Magdalena

because we are beyond wishing
folding prayers like paper airplanes
no, the time has come to storm heaven

until the gods weep at the sight
of the horses' bare backs

and become flesh, and ride
and ride and ride

*A milagro, which means miracle in Spanish, depicts the object for which a miracle is sought, such as a crippled leg or money to buy a house.

Dionisio D. Martínez

THE PRODIGAL SON LOSES HIS WIFE

It's not what you think. They are walking in a crowd when she suddenly dissolves. Tired of looking, he tells himself she must have gone home. At home, he finds the children waiting, demanding to know where their mother is. Understandable, he thinks, but he's sure she's on her way back. It was a small crowd, after all, and she couldn't possibly have gone too far. But the children soon grow restless. There have been numerous reports lately of missing people suddenly showing up in a strange family. The children want to know if their mother is watering blue geraniums in someone else's terrace. They propose an all-out search, but the father becomes suspicious, believes that they want to plant in him whatever seeds of guilt they've managed to find around the house. He thinks they've been through his papers, in his pockets, and under his mattress. One day he cannot remember his wife. He sees the children and tries to find her face in theirs, but it does not come. He listens for her voice in the voices of the children and only hears the children.

THE PRODIGAL SON BUYS A NEW CAR

because he has outgrown the one he bought when he outgrew the motorcycle they gave him when he outgrew his feet. In the interim he has outgrown all his clothes, houses, marriages, his two children, and the one language he thought he had mastered. Briefly he worked as a banker, but decided to quit when he noticed that he was becoming too attached to the concept of saving. Now he refers to it as his "nice little job in the warehouse." In a recurring dream he's been having lately, he's wearing a suit and operating a forklift, moving pallets of money from one end of a warehouse to the other and back. Brand new bills, large bills, all neatly wrapped and stacked. Beats driving a brand new car, he says.

STARFISH

That's not rain; it's a starfish constellation falling. When we go fishing we just hold out

our hands like nets. I wash them in salt
and they turn into islands. Trees sprout

from my lifelines. They taught me that clouds
are vapor that escapes from the water and rises

only to fall again. Like most island stories, this one
goes unquestioned. We will pry

open your starstruck, star-filled hands one
day. Let them clutch a little light while they

can. Clouds are helium islands, floating,
unbelievable as the sky itself. Let this be

your story, your amulet of words, the only magnet
that guides your compass across a starless continent.

—*for Jessica Marie Cason*

Julio Marzán

THE TRANSLATOR AT THE RECEPTION
FOR LATIN AMERICAN WRITERS

Air-conditioned introductions,
then breezy Spanish conversation
fan his curiosity to know
what country I come from.
"Puerto Rico and the Bronx."

Spectacled downward eyes
translate disappointment
like a poison mushroom
puffed in his thoughts as if,
after investing a sizeable
intellectual budget, transporting
a huge cast and camera crew
to film on location
Mayan pyramid grandeur,
indigenes whose ancient gods
and comet-tail plumage
inspire a glorious epic
of revolution across a continent,
he received a lurid script
for a social documentary
rife with dreary streets
and pathetic human interest,
meager in the profits of high culture.

Understandably he turns,
catches up with the hostess,
praising the uncommon quality
of her offerings of cheese.

FOREIGN HEART

The redneck bartender
yells out "Like the singer
guy in Spanish?" This
intercepts all eyes

from the Army-Navy Game.
So what am I doing there,
Upstate, besides the beer.
"Laundry across the street."

Country smiles all around.
Linda would say "Maybe
you're just mistaking."
Maybe. Hate mysteries.

Beyond these rites,
the Hudson River Valley.
Next spring I will be
Forty years a foreigner.

Víctor Montejo

SIN EL REZADOR

Algún día, en el futuro
ya no habrán alcaldes rezadores
ni guías que enseñen los caminos
o que ordenen los días y las horas
en el ciclo del tiempo.
Entonces el día de la justicia
se asomará a los pueblos
y habrán homicidios constantes,
destrucción de la tierra
e inundaciones.
La mano que protege al pueblo
se habrá levantado
y la gente desesperada gritará,
"¡Qué rece el rezador!"
pero el rezador, el mediador,
habrá enmudecido.

WITHOUT THE PRAYER-MAKER

One day, in the future
there will be no more prayer-makers
or guides who will reveal the paths
and place in order the days and the hours
in the cycle of time.
Then, the day of justice
will arrive in the towns;
there will be homicides everywhere
and the land will be eroded
by floods and landslides.
The hand which protects the people
will have already been lifted
and the desperate people will cry out,
"Let the prayer-maker pray!"
but the prayer-maker, the mediator
will already be voiceless.

Translated by the author

Pat Mora

HONDURAN GHOSTS

They look like ghosts,
Ohio at Halloween,
remind me of pumpkins, corn stalks, witches flying,
skeletons suspended to remind us
of the bones within. Hundreds, thousands,
of faceless forms hang white
row after row, perhaps the careful work
of hands at play, stretching each plastic bag
into the breeze, fields of dangling figures
for children eager for fright.

But no. No hands at play
on these plantations,
hands dark as earth work to prune
bananas, green fingers,
to toss the weak away
as mulch and pamper the chosen "hijos,"
ripening unblemished in all these plastic bags,
never touched by even a leaf, fed and checked,
weighed and measured and washed
to sweeten on the sea.

In this ripe country, children thin as twigs
sleep on street corners, their mouths full
of their own fingers.

Rosario Morales

LAST RITES

He was dying. She knew it. He no longer denied it. You'd think she would treat him to acceptance, to indulgence, to anything-you-want-dear, in his last six months. But it was her last six months too and she wanted to know, now, more than ever, what he thought, wanted more, not less, than ever to know what made him angry. She wanted the intimacy she'd always wanted, the easy flow of sharing, not the silence and sulks, not the tolerable misery of clotted desires and anger. So she pressured him, quarreled with him, abused him, reasoned with him. And because he was dying, because he wanted, and knew he deserved, the privilege of pity and tears and tiptoeing around him, because he wanted to be treated like a dying man, he was shocked and furious and for once fought back. They lived in a torment of contention, a daily strife shot through with brilliant moments of an almost unnatural, naked, tender intimacy, where his selfhood shone through his eyes with a golden light, where sudden bright bursts of joy wakened him from his ever more frequent drugged sleep. He died in a fever of eager disputation, rehearsing what to say next, impatient to contradict her, ask her, explain to her, to tell her what he thought, felt, wanted, life moving so strongly through him that he almost, but just almost, didn't die.

Elizabeth Pérez

WRITING MY WILL

We will live here, my father and I,
until the rent comes due, then move to another hotel.
Six feet above my bed
a pair of denim jeans straddles the ceiling lamp,
muting its one good bulb while I read
and singeing the unintentional holes
in the knees.
My papercut,
the one wound saliva was said to heal,
stings when I put a page to thumb.
Pain, no doubt, but tonight
no blood.

My father has snorted himself asleep again,
the shell of his eyelids thinner
than the sheer linen sheets
I hurl to my calves in the summer.
When he falls out of bed,
the door of my room screeches ajar.
I wait for him to thunder blasphemies
and flood my lungs
with the tinny aroma of Cuban rum.

Insomniacs do dream, he whimpered at dinner.
With teeth hairy
from scraping clean a mango seed,
he screamed about the parents who called him
"lightbulb shitted by blowflies"
for the motes of melanin
which littered his complexion.
My father dreams of himself as a moon,

of pox scars which thin to the blue lines
on a looseleaf page
and remembers being sponged
with lime juice and alcohol,
how affluent mulatto parents
readied their sons for parochial school.

I school myself.
My dingy blonde hair, the color of *guano bendito*,
falls in strips on the leatherbound encyclopedia,
a gift from the American grocery on the corner.
I reread the middle letters of the alphabet
to forget
the menace of guttural slumber,
the nip of pesticide on underripe tomatoes,
the futile search for roaches in vacant cabinets.
I cannot teach such experience
or document us refugees
with the splinters in my thumbs, so
to the next child, tenant, reader,
I leave bloody fingerprints for cursive letters
in lieu of pencil or paper.

THE ASSUMPTION

"La que no tiene del Congo, tiene del Caribali"

We have an ancestor descended
of true African royalty.
Asunción, qui a parlé français.
Asunción, new to Cuba,
at last brought Spanish words
out of the foreign plot of the tongue,
learned to lay a table and to sponge the slop
of a home that flowed with rum and sugar.
Hired by a wealthy diplomat,
Asunción wed his son after three years
of pidgin courtship.
At fifteen, under cubes of camphor
in the medicine drawer,
I found the photograph of their heir, Emiliano,
a shade lighter than whipped espresso,
the bow of his full lips
the whittled twig of a plantain plant.
As I teared, my aunt declared it
an article of faith
that Asunción
was not an escaped Haitain slave,
but of noble Congolese blood,
that she died fat and happy.
The portrait has since disappeared,
bísbísabuelo Emiliano stolen
by his great great granddaughter,
amber prescriptions and tools of exorcism
left mute on the shelf.
All my aunt said, eyes hard as thunderstones,
was *"Lo pierderas."* You'll lose it.

Now, whether I recover shreds of the portrait
bubbled under eggshells and coffee grounds,
or the corpse
of my great great grandfather
buried in the hollow belly of the cellar,
we are lost.
I run to you, M'Asunción,
caught between the hull of a ship
and the discreet white conclusion to your rape.
The life of your Congo now gone,
your tribal elite bargained North,
all I have of you are irises the color of pupils
and a gene that retards the healing of scars.
But what right have I to carry more?
Jésus-Christ, how strong a strength
could raise your own invisible wounds to fire?
Where are you? What does the fire eat?
And if I pray, what choice have I
but to call you "M'Asunción"
as I was told your owners did,
so you would feel at home,
because it sounded French?

Leroy Quintana

ZEN—WHERE I'M FROM

A good door needs no lock,
yet no one can open it.
                    —LAO TSU

You simply have to admire how, immediately after
the twelve-foot-high chain link fence
crowned with coils of wicked barbed wire was
erected, the fence the City Council voted on
unanimously to guard against anyone ever again,
again breaking into one of the town's
storage sheds, how immediately after, the
thieves drove up with their welding torches and
stole it!

HUBCAPS AND HI-FI

Lencho had a pretty nice '53
green Chevy, dice dangling
from the rear-view mirror;
this was in 1962
and here's how:

He wanted some nice spinners
so he posted me, because I
wasn't the boldest, as
lookout while he and
Tony deftly pried some
off a car quickly with
a screwdriver downtown
behind the El Rey Theater.

And when he wanted Hi-Fi
speakers for the back
he simply snipped two
from their posts right
after a double feature
at the Cactus Drive-In.

WHAT IT WAS LIKE

If you want to know what
it was like, I'll tell you
what my tío told me:
There was a truck driver,
Antonio, who could handle a
rig as easily in reverse as
anybody else straight ahead:

Too bad he's a Mexican was
what my tío said the
Anglos had to say
about that.

And thus the moral:

Where do you begin if
you begin with if
you're too good
it's too bad?

Bessy Reyna

LUNCH WALK

He came bouncing down the street
heavy body, long hair, jacket and tie
there was an oddness about him
then, as he approached
I heard the sound of maracas
coming from his pockets
—was it candy?
I pictured hundreds of multi-colored sweets
crashing against each other
he, oblivious to the crackling rhythm.

Along Capitol Avenue
our paths crossed
lunch break nearly over.
How can I explain
being late for work
because I was following a man
who sounded like maracas?

Luis J. Rodríguez

THE OLD WOMAN OF MÉRIDA

The old woman stares out an open window,
shards of sunlight pierce her face
cutting shadows on skin. She's washing
her hands after the dishes, dipping them
into a sea of hues and shapes,
a sea of syllables without sound,
in a stone house in Mérida,
her Mérida of dense México.

The water is a view to a distant place:
Kitchen walls fall to reveal a gray sky,
an array of birds in flight through fog—
the crushed white of waves curling at feet.
There appears a woman in forested hair,
eyes of black pearl,
who touches the hewn face of a man
and palms that feel like bark.
She winches at its blemishes
and something in her careens
against the walls of her heart.
She never wants to let go,
never wants to stop tracing
the scars above his eyebrows,
the tattoos on blackened skin,
while the lick of a tongue
stirs the night inside her.

The old woman looks at water and into
this vision shaped into a mouth—
the mouth of the sea that swallowed
her sailor-husband
so many sunlit windows ago.

Raúl R. Salinas

POEMA DEL NUEVO LEÓN

S
e
n
t a d o
e   m
n   i

favorite restaurant
surrounded by carnitas
y coronas
me pongo a platonear.

Meanwhile . . .
en un booth by the bar
Gloria (la waitress
especial) sits smiling
whiling away
minutes before her
shift/ swiftly munching
on a bunch of
(what i hope are
farmworker-friendly,
    pesticide-free,
       pro-Union!)
Grapes.

   —*austin, 1986*

A WALK THROUGH THE CAMPO SANTO

i walked through the Campo Santo of my ciudad tonight
visiting friends and relations playmates from childhoods
hurried/lived other mates from capitalist caves request stop
machinery for a while share in the sacred plants spreading the
presence of peace above/beneath the earth birthrights given
up the Spirit rusty nail at the heel locks the jaws locomotive
wheels become meat grinders the plague in the colony gang-
land guns coming and going family feud with his pistol in his
hand jazz trumpets blare flares catch the glimmer of the gun
running partner my blood of no more sounds no smoke-em-
ups narco hollow points riddled back .357 magnum reigns
stickpins in the skin pop poisonous veins 12 gauge shotgun
in the mouth scattered brains become wall designs life left
dangling on the old homestead backyard live oak tree elders
those who checked out caught the bus all on they own / popos
and grandpas grandmother gabriela dead not dead bracing up
temper the steel softening of the machine priestly eulogies
She Gave Birth to a Nation! an indio poet smiles and matriar-
chal voices set the tone as six generations sheep lonely in their
assimilation slump on cold, wooden church pews scratching
they heads wonder what it was the preacher meant bent on
knee i honor primos y tías compas & comrades shoulder to
shoulder laid out beneath caliche stones on sacred ground
i walked through the campo santo of my ciudad tonight.

—*austin, 1989*

Gary Soto

POMPEII AND THE USES OF OUR IMAGINATION

Our history teacher, a southern fellow,
Said, "Close your eyes
And think back, back, back . . ."
This was a new way of sleeping
In an 8 o'clock class, the sun a pink scar
In our eastern window. He told us about Pompeii,
A bad-luck city, and how lava ran over the poor
And the rich alike. Since I was between
A "B" and an inflated "A," I did what I was told.
I closed my eyes and imagined a huge tamale
Run over by *mole* sauce, my only reference
To a thing that got smothered. On top of this tamale,
A chariot, crowned Gods, an emperor in a white robe.
There was a slave and slave's bloody ax.
Then there was a Niña, Pinta and Santa María,
The wrong century. I wiped out this image
And returned to the flow
Of lava—jugs of wine, leather sandals, horses.
I saw a fountain, oxen, pigs and, for a second,
A covered wagon plugged with burning arrows.
My history was mixed up. I closed my eyes tighter,
And I returned to the lava flow—
Statues crumbling to their knees
And citizens caught in the hot river,
Their legs in the air. I saw virgins run
From the fire, soldiers in leather skirts and plumed helmets,
And then the covered wagon reappeared with more arrows.
My God, I scolded myself, What is wrong with you?
The history teacher repeated, "back, back, way back,"
I pulled together a harp, a bowl of grapes, figs like scrotums,
And then on the tamale I saw two cavemen,

No, three, all with faces of actors—
Yul Brynner, Tony Curtis, and Kirk Douglas,
My heroes! They were going to fight the lava,
Push it back. But they slipped on the *mole* sauce
And slipped away on the lens of my tears.
I had gone too far. I was no good at history.
The covered wagon floated behind my closed eyes,
Then an astronaut, then George C. Scott.
I couldn't think right. A fork then rose and fell
On that tamale, the steam uncurling,
Not unlike Pompeii when the land cooled,
Waves crashed, dogs sniffed the ruins,
And—my god—the covered wagon with Moses
And Charleton Heston struggling for the wheel!

THE ESSAY EXAMINATION FOR WHAT YOU
HAVE READ IN THE COURSE WORLD RELIGIONS

From his cross Jesus said, Sit up straight,
And Buddha said, Go ahead and laugh, big boy,
And although no god, Gandhi said, Do onto others . . .
The last one didn't seem right. I relicked my pencil
And looked out the classroom window—two dudes smoking joints,
Yukking it up while I was taking a timed exam.
I noticed a stray dog nosing a paper bag,
Which prompted me to look down at my feet—
My own lunch bag with three greasy splotches.
That was Pavlov, the reaction thing,
And at any moment I could start salivating.
I returned to my exam. I had to concentrate
And wrote, Zoroastrianism was a powerful religion
In a powerful time. Of taoism, I wrote,
The split personality made you more friends.
I liked my progress. I looked out the window again—
The two hippie dudes now petting the dog
And blowing smoke into its furry face. I wrote:
Confucius was a good guy who stroked his whiskers.
I stalled here. The last part didn't seem right,
And it didn't seem right that our teacher
Should be reading the sports page while we suffered.
I got back to work. Who was Shiva?
When did Shinto start? Why did the roofs of the pagodas
Swing upward? The rubbings from my eraser snowed
To the floor and my tongue was black as plague.
The clock ate up the hour. The teacher put down
His newspaper and said, You've been good students.
After class I went around to see the hippie dudes,
Now passed out against the wall. The dog lay

Between them, also snoozing, the joint smoldering
Next to his furry face. Unlike Gandhi
I didn't have much to say on the matter,
I opened my lunch bag with no judgment, no creed,
No French philosophical *nada*. I ate
A hog of a burrito and then the ancient, mealy fruit,
The apple of our first sin.

MOVING OUR MISERY

If we peed into a canal,
If we added our youthful lash of salts to the water,
Misery would carry itself out of town.
I had been reading philosophy for World Religions
And concluded we were in big trouble.
Pericles was long dead, Socrates a rag in the earth,
And Galileo the lunar grit under a farmer's thumbnail.
One day, when a girl said, No, I love you as a friend,
I took my sorrow and cried into this canal,
My Buddha-shaped tears falling like an ancient rain.
The canal moved, just slightly, stirred the dead water.
I unzipped there and it flowed—
The junk on the bottom, the sofas and tires,
A wagon wheel, fishing tackle, a telephone booth,
A yellow dish glove pointing toward heaven.
The water flowed, and right there I needed my brother,
Three of his husky friends, maybe one dog,
A circus elephant. What was philosophy
But youthful water on an ancient current?
We could count one,
Two, three, then unleash ourselves
Into the canal
Until it flowed like the Nile,
Flowed through yellowish vapors.
Then it would snow,
Maybe rain, and the fish would return,
An egret or a smirking duck, all of nature at our feet,
Some of it climbing into our hair—
The cricket kick starting the night in our left ear.
We are, my friend, looking at the Garden of Eden,
Where Man walked nobly in front of the lion,
But jumped a step when the beast roared at his tasty bottom.

Virgil Suárez

THE WOOD SCULPTOR

It could have been any medium:
clay, metal, glass, paint, paper—
he chose wood. So he sits on
a steel stool, back bent, rough hands
steady some of the time as he holds
a piece of wood. Seventy three &
he still craves the smoothness
of wood, its firm constitution,
ah its celestial scent of atoms
gathered to solidify. At night
he stays up & works best
between the hours of 12 & 5—
the most important work done
later rather than earlier; sometimes
he looks up and away from the work
to listen to the distant crow of a rooster,
every morning, the same rooster,
he's accepted the sound as a personal
greeting. Tonight like many nights
past he is intent on his wood, the only
sculpture he's been working on
since the beginning, a magnificent
replica of his garage wood shop
dusty windows, cracked walls,
greasy doorknobs, and all,
all carved out of wood.
He knows every contour.
He has sculpted
a tool chest & the dented Coca-Cola

can on top of it, the rusty screws
created too out of the same wood
along with the yellow handle
screwdrivers, chisels, hammers,
silver nuts & bolts, the red spray
paint can. There is even a piece
of black chain & some rope
he left hanging from the ceiling.
When he finishes this,
the world will seem whole; perfect.
He carves a replica of his Craftsman
drill press, the router, the jigsaw.
The trashcan by his table with dirty
sawdust inside. The GE light bulb
that hangs over his head, switch
& all. His books on carpentry.
Some day soon
he wants to make his apron
that hangs behind the door.
Oh the wood, wood like his worn
hands, blistered, cracked & scarred.
His eyes focus hard on the work
as he knows the way to make the wood
talk, come alive. He won't give up
until he's done with everything.
Sometimes he looks up from the wood
& gazes at nothing in particular, sighs,
daydreams. Like a blind man,
his fingers deciphering what the ridges
& notches on the wood say.
He has a thought just now,

profound & different:
If you take a mirror & prop it up
against another mirror,
there you can capture infinity,
so he takes his carving tools
& turns to work on the perfect
image of himself: of a man, as he
sits on a steel stool, back bent,
hands, not steady, buzzing
like insects over the wood.

XAGUA CASTLE, CIENFUEGOS

Sits on top of a high cliff overlooking the bay in which the docked boats stretch & dry their nets. The child stares at it from the balcony of some relative's house. His grandmother is there with him. She rocks on a wicker rocking chair behind him & tells him about the treasures Cook's pirates hid in the castle long ago. "Will you take me to see them?" the child asks. "Maybe tomorrow. It's too late & the ghosts are taking care of it now." The child asks if his grandmother was alive when they built the castle. She tells him no & takes his hand. "I wasn't born yet. The Spaniards built it." The child asks who the Spaniards were, were they good? Sometimes, she tells him, sometimes they didn't understand other people. The other people were the indians. The indians *were* the noblest of people. They didn't bother anyone, lived free to hunt & raise their families. "I want to see the ghosts," the child says. The grandmother assures him that if he looks hard enough he can see them from here. She smooths the wrinkles on her dress, gets up, and goes inside. The child sits with his legs dangling between the wrought-iron bars of the veranda while he admires the castle. The darker it grows, the more he believes he can see ghosts floating in & out of the high towers.

Gloria Vando

BASES LOADED

At
the
ballgame
people who
have never uttered
one kind word to one
another hug and kiss, hop up
and down, and scream with ethnic
abandon. Fans weep and blame each
other for losses they seem to feel more keenly
than death. A heavy-set woman in the third row
winds up and slugs her son because he shouts *hurray*
and claps his little hands when her shortstop fumbles. She is
oblivious of his pain at this first hit—the thud of bat against
ball, fist against skull fused in his future forever. The
woman next to my husband grabs his knee and
squeezes with the passion of a double. He
responds to the momentary pass by
squeezing back, his face flushed
with the anticipation of a
home run, the dread
of a triple play
just a batter
awa
y.

HE 2-104: A TRUE PLANETARY NEBULA IN THE MAKING

On the universal clock, Sagan tells us,
we are only moments old. And this
new crab-like discovery in Centaurus,
though older by far, is but
an adolescent going through a vital
if brief stage in the evolution
of interacting stars. I see it
starting its sidereal trek
through midlife, glowingly complex—
"a pulsating red giant" with a "small
hot companion" in tow—and think
of you and me that night in August
speeding across Texas in your red
Mustang convertible, enveloped in dust ·
and fumes, aiming for a motel bed,
settling instead for the backseat of the car,
arms and legs flailing in all directions,
but mostly toward heaven—and now
this cool red dude winking at me
through the centuries as if to say
I know, I know, sidling in closer
to his sidekick, shedding his garments,
shaking off dust, encircling
her small girth with a high-density
lasso of himself, high-velocity
sparks shooting from her ringed
body like crazy legs and arms until
at last, he's got his hot companion
in a classic hold and slowly,
in ecstasy, they take wing and
blaze as one across the Southern skies—
no longer crab but butterfly.

Clemente Soto Vélez

ESTOS ÁRBOLES

Estos árboles
no cosen
con madejas de nubes
el delantal del aire,
sino con hojas de canción
que mueven
brisas hilanderas;
no desatienden
la llamada próspera
del aire que hace esquina
olfateando su anhelo;
no desatienden
la fruta en sazón
que se mira
en el espejo del ombligo.

Estos árboles
no pasan por alto
—en el telar de la meditación—
a los que se acuestan de pie
caminando entre llamas;
no van
a los ocasos que desechan la aurora,
sino a los manzanares
que dan paso a la aurora
dentro de la transformación
juvenil del ocaso.

Estos árboles
no ignoran
que la lluvia

THESE TREES

These trees
do not sew
the air's apron
with a tangle of clouds,
but with leaves of song
that move
the threaded breezes;
do not ignore
the flourishing call
of the air that waits on the corner
sniffing for its deepest desire;
do not ignore
the ripened fruit
watching itself
in the mirror of the navel.

These trees
—on meditation's loom—
do not miss
the ones who sleep while standing,
walking through the flames;
do not go
toward the sunsets that shed the dawn,
but to the apple orchards
opening a path for dawn
inside the adolescent metamorphosis
of sunset.

These trees
do not ignore
the fact that the rain

voltea los horizontes
verdes del entendimiento
para transformar lo estéril
en atracción de altura.

Estos árboles
no dejan de comprender
que la corriente del raciocinio
no sube por el curso de su altura
—hasta llegar a ser nube—
echándose de menos a sí misma;
no dejan de comprender
que las aguas
que corren hacia arriba
miran a su declive
desde abajo;
no dejan de comprender
que el incendio congelado
del pensamiento
trabaja en la palabra
llena de palabra,
aserrando la madera
de su nombre.

Estos árboles
no dejan de oír
la primavera
que, dando estallidos inaudibles,
deshiela
la lozanía de su propósito
cargada de pimpollos venideros.

overturns the green horizons
of understanding
to transform sterility
into a magnetic height.

These trees
never cease to understand
that the current of reasoning
does not rise over the course of its height
—until it becomes a cloud—
longing for its missing self;
never cease to understand
that waters
which run upstream
watch their descent
from below;
never cease to understand
that the frozen fire
of thought
labors in the word
full of word,
sawing the wood
of its name.

These trees
never cease to hear
the spring
triggering inaudible explosions,
thawing
the lushness of its purpose
full of emerging blossoms.

Estos árboles
se amanecen
desmotando designios
en el sur del corazón,
para aconsejarse con las aguas
que se sumergen
antes de llegar a mojar
los labios
que predicen su llegada;
se amanecen
trabajando bien cerca de su voz,
con la buena intención
de estar lejos de ella,
descubriendo
lo que quiere pensar la madrugada;
se amanecen
ayudando a la ternura
endurecer sus pasos,
para no menoscabar
la inocencia de su madurez;
se amanecen
descendiendo
por la ascensión de su tortura
para entender
lo que deja de entender
la lengua
que va delante de sus llamas.

Estos árboles
se amanecen
desistiendo de seguir siendo
malmirados
por los que han de llegar
a entrar en sí mismos

These trees
that awaken
to dust off designs
in the southland of the heart,
divining the waters
which immerse themselves
before wetting
the lips
that foretell her arrival;
that awaken
working intimately with her voice,
remaining distant from her
with good intentions,
discovering
the thoughts of early morning;
that awaken
helping tenderness
to harden its steps,
so as not to diminish
the innocence of its maturity;
that awaken
descending
through the ascension of their torture,
to understand
what the tongue forgets
as it goes ahead of the flames.

These trees
awaken
refusing the continous
contempt
of the ones who will
possess themselves

después que el tiempo pierda
la validez de su medida;
se amanecen
descendiendo en su ascensión
para escuchar la tierra,
desvistiendo su sombra,
hojeando su decir;
se amanecen
al pie de su palabra
que, después de estar muerta,
se aventura a pensar
en su vivir.

Estos árboles
desamarran
la persuasión
en los puertos que tocan,
para que el mar descargue
sus metales de espumas,
para que los litorales
echen renuevos
de abrazos extendidos
en las olas que alzan
playas entre los dientes,
para que la arena
desenrede
la niebla de las costas,
mientras el entendimiento
se pone a desgajar
racimos de cariño,
para que los que duermen
oigan el sueño
tocarles a sus puertas

after time loses
the accuracy of its measure;
awaken
descending into their ascent
to listen to the earth,
stripping its shadow,
leafing through its speech;
awaken
at the foot of their word
that dares to contemplate
the act of living
even after death.

These trees
unleash
persuasion
in the harbors that touch,
so the sea can spew
its foam of metal,
so the shores
can sprout shoots
of welcoming arms
in the waves that lift up
beaches between their teeth,
so the sand
can untangle
the fog of the coastlines,
as understanding
unravels
clusters of affection,
so the sleepers
can hear the dream
knocking at their doors

antes de que la pesadilla
se sacuda los dedos
contando
a los sobrevivientes
por la unidad despierta de sus ojos.

Estos árboles
no incurren
en la indignación
de los puertos cerrados,
porque la tripulación de la paz
deja oír su canto de paloma
acompañada
por el mar
en el teclado de las aguas;
porque
la musicalidad
del ir en el venir
sale a tomar el aire
que renueva sus huesos.

Estos árboles
sienten relinchando
la impresión de la yerba rastrera
cerca del tallo tierno
donde el desencanto
cautiva su extinción;
sienten encenderse
a la queja
que sorprende su retrato
en la alegría
que no sabe por qué
la risa se queda pensando
en el balcón.

before the nightmare
shakes its fingers
counting
the survivors
through the awakened union of its eyes.

These trees
do not engage
in the indignation
of blockaded harbors,
because the crew of peace
lets its dove-song be heard
accompanied
by the ocean
on the keyboard of the waters;
because
the musicality
of leavetaking in return
emerges to draw the breath
renewing its bones.

These trees,
neighing, sense
the creeping vine
approaching the tender stalk
where disillusion
captures its extinction;
sense the illumination
of a grievance
that surprises its own portrait
amid jubilation
not knowing why
laughter lingers thoughtfully
on the balcony.

Estos árboles
le dan alberque
a la opinión desamparada
que tan elocuentemente
cultiva la anonimia
donde la madera verde de la lluvia
les brota en llamaradas
por los dedos;
porque
cuando comienzan a madurar
las mazorcas del júbilo
los sembradores sienten
en la ansiedad
de sus dedos anaranjados
desprendimientos de metáforas.

Estos árboles
se comunican con la doncella
que está con dolores
para que multiplique
el número de su amante
por sí misma,
para que pueda decir:
amado,
multiplícate
dentro de mí
para cuando la emoción
se acerque a su cuadrado
tu imaginación
cautive
la palabra con labios.

These trees
give shelter
to the abandoned opinion
which cultivates anonymity
so eloquently,
where the green wood of the rain
bursts into flames
through the fingers;
because
when the corn of jubilation
begins to ripen
the farmers sense
the shattering of metaphors
in the anxiety
of their orange-stained fingers.

These trees
speak to the virgin
in labor
multiplying
her lover's number
by her own,
so that she might say:
lover,
multiply yourself
inside me
so when emotion
is nearly squared
your imagination
can then capture
the word with your lips.

Estos árboles
se adentran
el las riberas púberes
del deleite
donde el mar y la tierra
se separan juntándose;
donde los enamorados
dejan su cuerpo atrás
para saber que se aman
antes de haberse amado;
donde el corazón
se sale a palpitar afuera,
donde la libertad
no desempeña
el rol de prisionera,
donde la libertad
es tierra
transustanciada en pétalos,
donde la libertad
plantea
su autoliberación,
donde la libertad
se mide
su conciencia de amante.

These trees
take root
in the pubescent riverbanks
of delight
where the ocean and the earth
separate at the moment of union;
where lovers
leave the body behind
knowing that they love each other
before having been loved;
where the heart
goes palpitating outside the body,
where liberation
does not play
the role of prisoner,
where liberation
is earth
transubstantiated into petals,
where liberation
advocates
its own liberation,
where liberation
is measured
by the consciousness of her lover.

Translated by Camilo Pérez-Bustillo and Martín Espada

Michael Veve

SERVICE ECONOMY FANTASTIQUE

After the
lights are   turned off at the
                    restaurant,
         the
                grillcook and dishwasher
                wait for the floor they have
                mopped to dry in the dark to the
                humid ministrations of eight ceiling
                fans and two stereo speakers
                pulsing like the throat of
                Marvin Gaye calling

         GET-UP GET-UP GET-UP GET-UP

         as
         they wait
         in dining room darkness,
         dancing in place before the Nero
         neon of the clock on the wall,   as the   windows
                                                blush.

THE BUSBOY SAW THIS

one night of the week
at the restaurant,
the waitresses
scrape the cadavers
of the 72 stale pastries
left out for show
into the jet glistening maw
of blind glad bags,
sag-bellied
with unchewed food.

Tino Villanueva

EN EL CLAROSCURO DE LOS AÑOS

Alertado vigía de mí mismo
me he parado
ante la noche insomne
a rechazar el sueño
cargado de memorias
que casi por sí solas
vanivienen
por los callejones de la infancia.
Qué manera de vivir
golpe a golpe
sintiéndome llamado a la exigencia
de pedir el sentido de las cosas.
Si me desvelo entre las sábanas
es que me relleva la torpeza
de no poder vencer
el despliegue denso de la noche,
de no poder contar cada suceso.

Vivir entonces
era acto perpetuo de confiar
el alma a los demás.
Y estoy viendo
en el claroscuro de los años
los sitios derramados que habité
con el tamaño bronceado
de mi cuerpo
y el alma hecha escombros
por el desdén
de los gobernantes en razón.

IN THE CHIAROSCURO OF THE YEARS

Vigilant, keeping watch on myself,
I've gotten up, insomniac
in the night,
to drive back
the memory-loaded dreams
that almost by themselves
come vainly
through the alleys of childhood.
What a way to live,
blow to blow,
feeling myself driven
to ask what things mean.
If I stay awake between the sheets
it's because I'm overcome
by my inability to conquer
the night's thick spread
and to account for each event.

Living then
was an endless act of trusting
my soul to others.
And in the chiaroscuro of the years
I'm seeing
the scattered places I lived in
with my fully
bronzed body
and soul turned to rubble
by the scorn of those
driving my mind.

Ahora el tiempo emerge
de las fechas requemadas
y de nuevo
se me notan los recuerdos
que estoy siendo.
Parece que no sirvo
más que para dar esta verdad . . .
aquí, yo, heredero
de todas mis memorias,
defendiendo a cada instante
la conciencia que antes me faltó.

Now the time
of the scorched days emerges
and again
the memories of what I'm feeling
come clear.
It appears my only function
is to give this truth . . .
here, I, heir
of all my memories,
defending each moment
the awareness I lacked before.

Translated by James Hoggard

SÓLO SÉ QUE AHORA

En el viento móvil
del recuerdo
soy los lugares apagados
donde he estado,
los soles
que me dejaron azonzado,
los cansancios infantiles
y su negación acorde.
Y pienso que quizás esta
solidaridad de palabras
no sea suficiente
para contar
tal y como entiendo el tiempo,
no sea suficiente
para entender
cómo el alma mide el tiempo atrás.
Sólo sé
que ahora que me veo
en la vereda que he formado
estoy conmigo y con mi todo,
reconozco
que todo cuanto he sido
espera en la memoria.
Las razones de esta historia
jamás podré abdicar.

I ONLY KNOW THAT NOW

In memory,
that moving wind,
I'm the muted places
where I've been,
I'm the suns
that stunned me,
the fatigue I felt as a child
and the diminishment that came with it.
And maybe
this solidarity of words
is inadequate
to tell all that
and, as is true in understanding time,
it's not enough
to understand
how soul measures past.
I only know
that now that I see myself
in the path I've made
I'm at home with myself and all that means,
I recognize
how much of all I've been
waits in memory.
And I could never walk away from
anything behind this story.

Translated by James Hoggard

Enid Santiago Welch

WELL-FARE WITH NO ADDRESS

The hot air is stuck to itself.
Hot muggy breeze.
    Walk to the bus stop.
No relief.
Eighty-five cents in a left pocket,
Wait to be gulped whole
By the fare-meter
Of the Pioneer Valley
Transit Authority's bus.

Welfare bound—Liberty Street
Appointment for re-determination.
Paperwork.
Signature.
        Bring proof.
Proof of residency—home,
trailer, apt., or mail box?
Proof of income: no address.
Proof of dependents: Yes, two.
They look like me.
Proof of bank accounts—no address.
Proof of utility bills—no address.
Proof of existence—yes, smell my
Cardboard skin.

Do you own stocks or bonds?
Repeat the question please?
Do you own any stocks or bonds?

No. No address.
How many persons live
In your home?
Three with no address.
Do you own a car? No.
Are you sure? Yes.
Sign here.
It's mandatory.

POPPING OUT BABIES WHILE DRAGGING YOUR PLACENTA TO THE MAIL BOX

Memo: To Newt G.

Open wide and sneeze
a child into existence.
Open wide and slide those
babies out.
Easy as A B C   pop.
Your belly enlarges.
Get in line   pop.
Can't wait for the check.
Ninety dollars a month more   pop.
There's no pain.
Just an in and out   pop.
A quickie   pop.
No pleasure   pop.
Just squeeze the infant out hard.
Push hard.
Don't stop.
Have to get to the mailbox fast.
Got to get that check cashed   pop.
Drag the placenta with you,
For ninety dollars a month more   pop.
Stretch-marks mapping
your skin,
Don't mind them at all.
And the morning sickness—all day   pop
Don't mind that.
The waddle-paddle walk and
the sleepless nights   pop.

The cervix opening
like a train tunnel   pop.
The feeling of a tree trunk
splitting you in half   crack crack
for ninety dollars extra
a month   pop.
Get a hysterectomy, complete   snip snip
not washed thin
like India ink in water,
blotched — pop.

Contributors' Notes

Martín Espada, from Brooklyn, New York, is the editor of this volume. He has published five collections of poetry, most recently *Imagine the Angels of Bread*, which won an American Book Award. He received the PEN/Revson Fellowship and the Paterson Poetry Prize for *Rebellion Is the Circle of a Lover's Hands*. He is also the editor of *Poetry Like Bread: Poets of the Political Imagination from Curbstone Press*. A former tenant lawyer, he is currently a professor of English at the University of Massachusetts, Amherst.

Pedro López Adorno, from Puerto Rico, has published various collections of poetry and edited the anthology *Papiros de Babel*. He is a professor of Black and Puerto Rican studies at Hunter College.

Marjorie Agosín, from Chile, has published numerous books of poetry, short fiction, critical studies, and, most recently, a memoir entitled *A Cross and a Star: Memoirs of a Jewish Girl in Chile*. She is the 1995 winner of the Letras de Oro Prize for Poetry and is a professor of Spanish at Wellesley College.

Jack Agüeros, from East Harlem, New York, is the author of a short story collection, *Dominoes*, and two poetry collections, *Correspondence between the Stonehaulers* and *Sonnets from the Puerto Rican*. He is also the editor and translator of Julia de Burgos, *Song of the Simple Truth: The Complete Poems*. He is former director of the Museo del Barrio in New York City.

Miguel Algarín's books of poetry include *Time's Now/Ya es Tiempo*, *On Call*, and *Love Is Hard Work*. He has also published *Action*, a collection of theater pieces. He is the founder of the Nuyorican Poets Café in New York City and is a professor of English at Rutgers University in New Brunswick, New Jersey.

Julia Alvarez, from the Dominican Republic, has published three poetry collections, *The Housekeeping Book*, *Homecoming*, and *The Other Side / El Otro Lado*, and three novels: *How the García Girls Lost Their Accents*, which won the PEN/ Oakland Josephine Miles Award; *In the Time of the Butterflies*, a National Book Critics Circle Award finalist; and, most recently, *¡Yo!* She is a professor of English at Middlebury College in Vermont.

Nicomedes Suárez-Araúz was born in the Amazonian region of Bolivia. He has published six books of poetry, including *Caballo al anochecer*, winner of Bolivia's national Premio Edición Franz Tamayo. His work has appeared in such anthologies as *Giant Talk* and *For Neruda, For Chile*. He presently teaches in the Spanish department at Smith College and is codirector of the Center for Amazonian Literature and Culture. He is also coeditor of *Amazonian Literary Review*.

Naomi Ayala recently published her first book of poems, *Wild Animals on the Moon*. She works with writing programs throughout the state of Connecticut.

Gioconda Belli was born in Nicaragua. She has published numerous works of fiction and poetry, including the best-selling novel *La mujer habitada/The Inhabited Woman* and *De la costilla de Eva/From Eve's Rib*, a collection of poetry. Her awards include Nicaragua's National University Poetry Prize and the Casa de las Américas Poetry Prize. A former combatant in the Sandinista revolution, she currently lives in Los Angeles.

Alicia Borinsky, from Argentina, teaches at Boston University. She has recently published two collections of poetry, *La pareja desmontable/The Collapsible Couple* and *Madres alquiladas* (Rent-a-Mom), and the novels *Sueños del seductor abandonado/Dreams of the Abandoned Seducer* and *Cine continuado* (All-night movie). She is the recipient of the 1996 Latino Literature Prize for Fiction.

Camilo Pérez-Bustillo is an attorney and translator living in Mexico City. The recipient of a Kellogg Fellowship, he is the cotranslator of *The Blood That Keeps Singing/La sangre que sigue cantando* by Clemente Soto Vélez.

Rafael Campo is the author of two poetry collections: *The Other Man Was Me*, winner of the National Poetry Series competition, and *What the Body Told*. He has recently published a memoir, *The Poetry of Healing: A Doctor's Education in Empathy, Identity, and Desire*. He is a practicing physician at Beth Israel Hospital and also serves on the faculty at Harvard Medical School.

Ana Castillo is a poet, fiction writer, and essayist. Her most recent books are *Massacre of the Dreamers: Essays on Xicanisma* and *Loverboys*, a collection of short stories. She lives in Chicago.

Sandra Cisneros is the author of several collections of poetry and short fiction, including *The House on Mango Street* and *Woman Hollering Creek*. She was recently awarded a MacArthur Fellowship.

Judith Ortíz Cofer is the author of six books, most recently *An Island Like You: Stories of the Barrio*. She received the Anisfield-Wolf Book Award for *The Latin Deli: Prose and Poetry*. She is a professor of English and creative writing at the University of Georgia.

Celeste Kostopulos-Cooperman has published a critical study, *The Lyrical Vision of María Luisa Bombal*, and has translated several books and poems from the Spanish, most recently *A Cross and a Star: Memoirs of a Jewish Girl in Chile* by Marjorie Agosín. She is a professor of modern languages and humanities and director of the Latin American studies program at Suffolk University.

Víctor Hernández Cruz is the author of many books of poetry and prose, including *Mainland, Snaps,* and *Red Beans*. He lives in Aguas Buenas, Puerto Rico, where he is currently finishing a novel.

Carlos Cumpián hails from San Antonio, Texas, and has spent half his life in Chicago trying to get back to his *Tejas*. He is the author of three poetry collections, *Coyote Sun, Latino Rainbow,* and *Armadillo Charm*.

Sandra María Esteves has published four volumes of poetry, most recently *Bluestown Mockingbird Mambo* and *Undelivered Love Poems*. She teaches poetry throughout New York City.

Rosario Ferré, from Puerto Rico, has published numerous works of fiction and poetry, including the poetry collection entitled *Antología personal*, as well as the novels *Sweet Diamond Dust* and *The House on the Lagoon*, which was a finalist for the National Book Award.

Cola Franzen has translated more than fifteen books from the Spanish, including works by Federico García Lorca and Jorge Guillén. Most recently, she has published a translation of *Mina cruel/Mean Broad*, a novel by Alicia Borinsky, as well as poems from Borinsky's collection, *La pareja desmontable/The Collapsible Couple*.

Diana García is from Merced, California. Her poems have appeared in such journals as the *Kenyon Review* and *Mid-American Review*. She currently teaches in the Department of English at Central Connecticut State University.

Magdalena Gómez has been widely anthologized in such collections as *Paper Dance: 55 Latino Poets* and *Working Days: Short Stories about Teenagers at Work*. Her most recent children's plays, *Latino Voices: Remembering* and *Another Way to See*, are currently touring New England schools with the Enchanted Circle Theater.

Ray González, author of five books of poetry and a book of essays, as well as editor of sixteen anthologies, has received the Before Columbus Foundation American Book Award for Excellence in Editing and a 1996 PEN/Oakland Josephine Miles Award for *The Heat of Arrivals*, a book of poems. He is a professor of English and Latin American studies at the University of Illinois in Chicago.

Juan Felipe Herrera's recent books of poetry include *Love after the Riots* and *Night Train to Tuxtla*. The recipient of three NEA Fellowships, he has also published *Mayan Drifter: A Chicano Poet in the Lowlands of America* and a bilingual children's book, *Calling the Doves*.

James Hoggard is the author of ten books, including four collections of poems, two novels, three collections of translations, and a collection of personal essays. Among his translations is the work *Chronicle of My Worst Years/Crónica de mis años peores* by Tino Villanueva.

Norberto James was born in the Dominican Republic. One of the most important voices of the Dominican Republic in the late 1960s, he published his first book of poetry, *Sobre la marcha*, in 1969. Since then he has published three more: *La provinca sublevada*, *Vivir*, and *Hago constar*. He has taught Spanish and Latin American literature in the Boston area. The poems included here will appear in his forthcoming book, *Cuaderno rojo*.

Rick Kearns is the author of one poetry collection, *Street of Knives*. He is the former editor of the literary magazine *Blue Guitar*, and has taught a course on poetry of protest at Rutgers University in New Brunswick, New Jersey.

Frank Lima was born in New York City in 1939. He has published three volumes of poems: *Inventory*, *Underground with the Oriole*, and *Angel*. *Inventory: New and Selected Poems* will be published in the fall of 1997. A fifth book, *IDoBelieveIDoBelieveIDoBelieve* is scheduled to be published in 1998. He teaches culinary arts at the New York Restaurant School.

Demetria Martínez is from Albuquerque, New Mexico. She won the Western States Book Award for her novel, *Mother Tongue*, which has been reissued by Ballantine. She has also published two poetry collections, *Turning* and *Breathing between the Lines*. She writes a column for the *National Catholic Reporter*.

Dionisio D. Martínez, born in Cuba, is the author of two poetry collections: *Bad Alchemy* and *History as a Second Language*. He has been the recipient of a National Endowment for the Arts Fellowship and a Whiting Writers' Award.

Julio Marzán is the author of *Translations without Originals*, a collection of poetry, and the editor-translator of *Inventing a Word: An Anthology of Twentieth-Century Puerto Rican Poetry*. He has also published a book of criticism, *The Spanish-American Roots of William Carlos Williams*.

Víctor Montejo is a Jakaltek Maya from Guatemala. He is the author of two poetry collections: *El Q'anil: Man of Lightning* and *Sculpted Stones*; a memoir,

Testimony: Death of a Guatemalan Village; and a collection of fables, *The Bird Who Cleans the World*. He is currently teaching in the Department of Native American Studies at the University of California, Davis.

Pat Mora, a native of El Paso, Texas, has published four books of poetry, most recently *Agua Santa: Holy Water*; a collection of nonfiction, *Nepantla: Essays from the Land in the Middle*; and a memoir, *House of Houses*. She has received a Kellogg Fellowship, a Southwest Book Award, and a National Endowment for the Arts Fellowship. A fifth book of poetry, *Aunt Carmen's Book of Practical Saints*, is forthcoming.

Rosario Morales has published *Getting Home Alive*, a collection of poetry and prose she wrote with her daughter, Aurora Levins Morales. Her work has been widely anthologized, appearing in such publications as *An Ear to the Ground*, *Cuentos: Stories by Latinas*, and *This Bridge Called My Back*.

Elizabeth Pérez, a Cuban American writer, has published in various journals, including the *Bilingual Review*. She is a recent graduate of Hampshire College and is currently a Mellon Fellow in Religious Studies at the University of Chicago Divinity School.

Leroy Quintana has published five poetry collections, including *Sangre* and *The History of Home*, each of which won an American Book Award. He is a professor of English at Mesa College in San Diego.

Bessy Reyna is the author of *She Remembers* and *Terrarium*, poetry chapbooks, and *Ab Ovo*, a collection of short stories. She has received awards from the Connecticut Poetry Society and the Connecticut Commission on the Arts. She is presently the editor of *El Extra Cultural*.

Joseph Rodeiro is an art historian, painter, and poet and the winner of a Fulbright Lecture Research grant for research in Nicaragua. He has translated the work of many Spanish American poets, including Pablo Neruda and Nicolás Guillén. He teaches at Jersey City State College.

Luis Rodríguez has published two volumes of poetry, *Poems across the Pavement* and *The Concrete River*, as well as a memoir, *Always Running: La Vida Loca, Gang Days in LA*. His awards include a Lannan Foundation Fellowship, a Lila Wallace – Reader's Digest Writers Award, and the Carl Sandburg Award.

Raúl R. Salinas is the author of three poetry collections: *Viaje/Trip*, *Un Trip through the Mind Jail*, and *East of the Freeway*. He lives in Austin, Texas, where he is the owner of Resistencia Bookstore/Casa de Red Salmon Press.

Gary Soto's most recent books are *Junior College, Canto Familiar,* and *New and Selected Poems,* a finalist for the National Book Award. In addition to poetry, he has written essays, short stories, and plays. He is completing the libretto "Nerd-Landia" for the Los Angeles Opera's Opera-in-the-High-Schools program.

Virgil Suárez, born in Cuba, has published four novels, *Latin Jazz, The Cutter, Havana Thursdays,* and *Going Under,* as well as a collection of stories entitled *Welcome to the Oasis.* Most recently he published a memoir titled *Spared Angola: Memories from a Cuban-American Childhood.* He is a professor in the creative writing program at Florida State University.

Gloria Vando is the author of a poetry collection, *Promesas: Geography of the Impossible,* a finalist for the Walt Whitman Award. She is the editor and publisher of Helicon Nine Editions in Kansas City, Missouri.

Clemente Soto Vélez (1905–1993) was a major Puerto Rican poet who published such works as *Caballo de palo/The Wooden Horse* and *La tierra prometida/The Promised Land.* He was imprisoned from 1936 to 1942 for his leadership role in the Puerto Rican independence movement.

Michael Veve won the Class of 1940 Poetry Award from the University of Massachusetts, Amherst.

Tino Villanueva, from San Marcos, Texas, has published four volumes of poetry, including *Scene from the Movie "Giant,"* which won a 1994 American Book Award. He teaches Spanish at Boston University.

Enid Santiago Welch has published widely in literary journals, including the *Bilingual Review,* the *Minnesota Review,* and *Peregrine.* She is an AmeriCorps Volunteer with Amherst Artists and Writers Institute.

Beth Wellington has published translations in various journals and anthologies, including the *New England Review and Bread Loaf Quarterly, Nimrod, Being América,* and *Remaking a Lost Harmony: Stories from the Hispanic Caribbean.* She received the Robert Fitzgerald Translation Award from Boston University. She is currently the director of the Center for Language and Culture at Babson College.

Steven F. White is a poet, editor, and translator. His poetry collections include *From the Country of Thunder* and *Burning the Old Year.* He has translated *From Eve's Rib* by Gioconda Belli, *A Poet in New York* by Federico García Lorca, and *The Birth of the Sun: Selected Poems* by Pablo Antonio Cuadra, among others. He is the recipient of a National Endowment for the Arts Translators Grant.

Acknowledgments

The following poems have been previously published in "El Coro: A Chorus of Latino/Latina Poetry," a special section of *The Massachusetts Review* 36, no. 4 (Winter, 1995-96) and are reprinted by permission of the authors, who hold copyright: Pedro López Adorno, "Liquid Matter" and "Talking to the Waves"; Marjorie Agosín, "Los desaparecidos"/"The Disappeared"; Jack Agüeros, "Psalm for Bacalao" and "Sonnets for the Four Horsemen of the Apocalypse: Long Time among Us"; Miguel Algarín, "Nuyorican One Wing Olive-Skin Angel"; Julia Alvarez, "The Way It Sounds," "The Dashboard Virgencita," and "The Lost & Found Señoritas"; Naomi Ayala, "Papo, Who'd Wanted to Be an Artist" and "Reform"; Alicia Borinsky, "Traición"/"Betrayal" and "Ocupaciones de la crítica"/"The Critics' Trade"; Ana Castillo, "El chicle"; Sandra Cisneros, "Tango for the Broom" and "It Occurs to Me I Am the Creative/Destructive Goddess Coatlicue"; Judith Ortíz Cofer, "The Tip"; Víctor Hernández Cruz, "Islandis" and "The Lower East Side of Manhattan"; Sandra María Esteves, "Puerto Rican Discovery #12: Token Views"; Rosario Ferré, "La sombra de la culpa"/"The Shadow of Guilt" and "Requiem"/"Requiem"; Magdalena Gómez, "La Terraza"; Ray González, "Ése," "The Cost of Family," and "These Days"; Juan Felipe Herrera, "Aphrodisiacal Dinner Jacket" and "The Anthropomorphic Cabinet"; Rick Kearns, "Aurelio's Vengeance, Puerto Rico, 1901" and "Jíbaros"; Demetria Martínez, "Imperialism," "We Talk about Spanish," and "Milagros"; Dionisio D. Martínez, "The Prodigal Son Loses His Wife," "The Prodigal Son Buys a New Car" (revised), and "Starfish"; Julio Marzán, "The Translator at the Reception for Latin American Writers" and "Foreign Heart"; Pat Mora, "Honduran Ghosts"; Leroy Quintana, "Zen—Where I'm From," "Hubcaps and Hi-Fi," and "What It Was Like"; Gary Soto, "Pompeii and the Uses of Our Imagination," "The Essay Examination for What You Have Read in the Course World Religions," and "Moving Our Misery"; Virgil Suárez, "The Wood Sculptor" and "Xagua Castle, Cienfuegos"; Clemente Soto Vélez, "Estos árboles"/"These Trees"; Michael Veve, "Service Economy Fantastique"; Tino Villanueva, "En el claroscuro de los años"/"In the Chiaroscuro of the Years" and "Sólo sé que ahora"/"I Only Know That Now"; and Enid Santiago Welch, "Well-Fare with No Address."

Copyrights to the poems that have been added to this edition are held by their authors.

"Voyage" by Pedro Lopéz Adorno was originally published in *Callaloo* 15, no. 4 (Fall 1992). Reprinted by permission of the author.